DAWN OF DECEPTION

Unbound, Book 1

A. R. SHAW

Copyright © 2018 by A. R. Shaw

Apocalyptic Ventures LLC

All rights reserved.

No part of this book may be reproduced in any form or by any electronic or mechanical means, including information storage and retrieval systems, without written permission from the author, except for the use of brief quotations in a book review.

For those of you, unbound.

FOREWORD

In a post-apocalyptic world, Sloane Delaney struggles to keep her daughters safe. With all her neighbors gone and her abusive second husband dead, Sloane and her daughters, Mae and Wren, maintain a dangerous charade to keep looters at bay from their neighborhood. When young Nicole shows up on their doorstep, nearly dead from dehydration and starvation as a result of her father's growing paranoia, she joins the determined group as they adjust to life without most of the luxuries they had previously taken for granted. Aided by a pack of abandoned dogs, the women are able to project an image of an occupied and active neighborhood until corrupt FEMA agents arrive on the scene, threatening their hard-won sense of security. Fleeing their now-unsafe home, Sloane and her girls head for the woods and an abandoned old house Sloane is sure will be a safe haven for at least a few days. She doesn't count on the handsome and helpful Dr. Kent having also taken refuge there. With her girls' lives on the line, can Sloane learn to trust again in this dangerous new world?

If you're going through hell, keep going.

— WINSTON CHURCHILL

I

Night before Dawn

Sloane Delaney and her daughters abandoned the first floor of their two-story home along Horseshoe Lane altogether. A tsunami wave—caused by a massive earthquake along the Pacific Rim—hit after some phenomena no one could yet explain, sending floodwaters that overtook their neighborhood situated in the once-picturesque setting of Cannon Beach, Oregon.

The displaced seawater had receded from the first floor, leaving an indelible layer of thick, brown, chocolate pudding-like sludge along the painted sandstone walls and Italian tiled flooring. The wayward sea currently hid at a lazy standstill below in the basement like a freeloading relative, getting stinkier by the day. It wasn't done with them yet. The basement was full of it, only having ebbed an inch since the day before.

And yet, on the queen-sized bed she used to share with Brady, Sloane slept in peace for the first night since the fateful day that she'd married him a few unpleasant years before. She wasn't worried about marauders storming the neighborhood or anyone breaking into her food stores like she should be. She hadn't even boarded up her blown-out sliding glass door yet. Any opportunistic person—or hungry animal, for that matter—could waltz into her disaster of a house and take everything left of value. Those worries could wait. Sloane wanted to enjoy the one solitary, peaceful night given to her because of what had happened to her husband earlier in the evening. Across the street, in the sodden backyard of Larry Baker's house, Brady lay dead—murdered, in fact, by a single gunshot wound to the head.

She wasn't the murderer, and she didn't plan it, yet she had *hoped* that it would happen. Brady had sent her, unwillingly, directly across the street to gather information on Trent Carson's plans to leave town, with several other neighbors, to a hideout he knew of.

Trent was guarded with his information. They'd been friends once, but that was before her marriage to Brady. None of her friends and neighbors liked Brady much, especially not Trent, and a short time after the marriage, she didn't like him either.

Then Sloane informed Trent of her own fake plans of heading to Hillsboro. She had hoped Trent would catch on to her hint when he advised her to be careful on Route 23. She told him she'd planned to take Route 30 instead. She and Trent both knew Route 30 didn't go anywhere near Hillsboro. Her act of going along with his advice was cunning desperation; she knew Brady was listening to her every word. Unfortunately, Trent didn't realize the ploy and ended up thinking she was in on Brady's mad plan to steal one of the few running vehicles from Larry Baker, Trent's next-door neighbor. Trent ended up shooting Brady in Larry's backyard that night when he'd refused to drop the shotgun he carried.

Immediately after taking Brady out, Trent hurried across the street to Sloane's driveway, warned her to stand down, and drop the concealed weapon he knew she carried onto the ground. "Is he dead?" she'd asked. That was really all she wanted to know.

"Yes," Trent said with what she'd call a little trepidation in his voice.

"Good," Sloane said and didn't care what Trent did to her for her part in Brady's scheme to rob her neighbors of their only working vehicle. Her only thought was that Brady being dead ensured her daughters' safety now. She no longer had to endure his mistreatment of her and the girls.

The verbal abuse started shortly after they were married. The threats and physical abuse escalated over the past year to include Sloane's sixteen-year-old daughter, Wren, and her thirteen-year-old daughter, Mae. She'd never forgive herself for not saving them sooner. They were already scarred from losing their father to a pandemic flu four years prior.

She was hospitalized in the ICU for weeks with the virus without knowing where her daughters were. When she finally escaped the hospital three weeks later as one of the lucky few to recover from the pandemic flu, she found her twelve-year-old and nine-year-old living alone in their house. Those were vulnerable years in a young girl's life in normal times, marred with insecurities and night frights. The Carsons and Bakers had done their best, under the circumstances, to keep track of them and bring them food. Unaccompanied and not knowing that their father had died or that their mother was desperately trying to get home to them, the girls were scared to death.

She was broken after Finn, her first husband, died. She felt utterly lost when she discovered that even her distant, extended family in Hillsboro had perished from the flu as well. So when Brady came along and offered stability as a family again, she did it for the girls' sake, thinking it was the right decision. She wanted to replace the things they'd lost. She wanted to fix them. Ultimately, her decision couldn't have been more wrong.

After Trent left her alone in the neighborhood the night before, she retrieved her Glock off the ground, returned to her home, and locked the main door. The girls had waited inside, so

Sloane ushered them up the stairs and into her own room. She locked the door and looked into their frightened eyes, which beckoned her for answers. "He's not coming back," she said. "He's gone for good."

All three of them cried tears of relief as they cuddled on the big bed, and Sloane held them until they fell soundly, and safely, asleep. Afterward, she remembered what Trent said to her before he left. *"Help yourself to anything you can salvage."*

She had responded with a thank you and said that, in return, she'd keep an eye on their houses. She knew what tomorrow and every other morning would bring to them, so she pushed herself into a peaceful slumber. There would be days of dreadful labor and danger ahead of her and the girls. If they were to survive this —and they would—she'd meet it willingly, and never again would she succumb to a weakness of mind or an empty soul to fill the void Finn's death left in her heart.

2

Daybreak

"Mmmooommm!" Mae whispered in a tone far too loud to be a whisper at all that ended up sounding ghostly. Sloane heard the plea from a deep and drowsy state, but what woke her was the moist breath sliding down like a hand over her nose and mouth. She sat up with a start, vaguely remembering the events of the previous night and how they might relate to the morning's dawn.

"What?" she said, confused, her heart pounding out of her chest. Her hand had already clasped around her daughter's forearm, and her brown eyes searched the room for her older daughter Wren. Once she saw her sitting nearby, Sloane's eyes flew to the door. *Was the bedroom door still locked?* It was closed, and the six white panels faced her, still as intact as the night before.

"Are you okay?" Sloane asked.

"Yeah," Mae said, startled that she'd scared her mother so badly.

"We were wondering when you'd get up," said Wren.

Sloane looked into Mae's sea-blue eyes, so much like her father's. "What time is it?"

"I don't know. There's no power, remember?" Mae reminded her.

She looked to Wren. "You haven't left the room, right?"

"No, Mom. We haven't left. We were waiting for you to wake up. It's really quiet out there," Wren said, reflecting Sloane's own brown eyes back to her.

She released Mae's arm with an apologetic look and a smile. "That's a sound I want you to both remember," she said, holding up a finger. "Listen to it. Remember that silence."

She held their gaze a moment. She'd been a high school French teacher before it all started, and teaching habits die hard. "Silence. That's what we need. Any sound we hear from now on is potential danger. Remember that," she said as she slipped her boots on over the cuffs of her jeans and slung a button-up chambray shirt over her white tank top. "Let's tidy up and have a bite to eat. We have a lot of work to do today...well, every day from now on."

She opened the nightstand drawer and pulled out her black Velcro thigh holster as her daughters readied themselves for the day. She slid the black waistband strap on her hips and looped the leg strap around the outside of her thigh. After placing the Glock from her nightstand into the harness, she checked the position for an easy reach.

This was one of the many lessons Trent and his wife Harper taught her after things calmed down from the pandemic, and they'd finally established a semblance of normal life—until now, of course. She'd been to the range once or twice a month and found that the Glock easily fit into her hands. She even enjoyed shooting, once she got past the phase of closing her eyes right before firing.

That was before she met Brady. Since then, she'd kept the gun to herself. She wasn't sure why. Something always told her to keep the weapon a secret from him, and she did. She'd dreamed about using it, more than once, to solve her problems when the abuse started. However, her daughters always sprang to mind, and since their father's death, they had no one in the world left alive but her. She couldn't risk abandoning them.

Sloane reached for her boar bristle brush and pulled it through her light-brown, shoulder-length hair. She then wrapped the extra length at the nape of her neck and looped it through an elastic band. Next, she went over to her dresser and pulled out her black, one-piece sports swimsuit. *This is going to be a long day,* she thought as she tossed it into a nylon bag and added a small, high-powered flashlight. She pulled the nylon cording tight and slipped it over her wrist.

Mae, already dressed and ready for the day, walked toward the door and was about to open it when Sloane cautioned, "No Mae, only I open the door. Wait for me, okay?"

"Sorry Mom," Mae said.

"Don't be sorry. Be safe," she said and internally groaned. She just couldn't help stating motherly advice. It happened automatically.

Sloane went to the window and looked outside. Not a soul was visible in the subdued early morning, blue-lit street. No candle lights remained on in the Carson's house across their driveway. No cars drove down the road. She couldn't see the rest of the neighborhood from her position in the master bedroom, but what she did see looked calm and quiet.

She headed for the door, stopped, waited, and listened—more to teach the girls about how vigilant they needed to be now than for any other reason. She opened the door a crack, barely making a sound, and stepped out. A crazy thought ran through her mind; perhaps Brady was waiting to get her. Just the thought sent her pulse racing. No longer willing to let him ruin what remained of their lives, she shoved the thought away as she forced her pulse to slow down.

Stepping lightly across the flood-ruined carpet, she walked into the upstairs loft. It used to be their library, where the girls would spend lazy afternoons working on puzzles when they were younger. In recent years, the space became a quiet escape for them to lounge on the overfilled sofa cushions, bobbing their heads to music attached to them with strings while pretending to read the classics their mother always insisted upon. Since it overlooked the main floor the room now served as their new kitchen and living area. Sloane walked over to the banister and looked over the railing while the girls hung back in the opened bedroom doorway.

She kept her hand hovering over her thigh holster. Looking below, she saw only their boot prints left in the hallway by the mudroom door from the night before. Nothing more. No one had tracked in through the busted sliding glass doorway in the living room, either.

"I think it's clear." She waved the girls toward her. "Wren, you get breakfast going while Mae and I bring the luggage back upstairs."

"Are you sure he's gone, Mom?" Wren whispered, clearly not willing to believe her mother yet.

She stopped her descent on the stairs and turned to answer her daughter, "Yes Wren, he's absolutely gone. We won't see him ever again. I promise."

Wren nodded to her.

"So we're staying here?" Mae asked with excitement.

"We are for now."

"Yay!" Mae cheered, and Sloane spun around on her jubilant daughter.

"Quiet, Mae! Let's keep our voices down to a whisper from now on. We can't let on that we live here alone. We have to make people believe there are many people living here, not just three ladies, or there could be trouble for us. Do you understand?" Sloane asked her, hoping she did. She knew Mae had the same feelings she did now that Brady was gone. The mental bindings Brady had bestowed upon them, making them feel like prisoners in their own home, were finally lifted and she too wanted to shout for joy. Hopefully, that chance would come in time; however, for now she needed to devise a way to keep them alive. Shouting and attracting attention to themselves was not the answer.

Her daughter's serious face told her she got it. "Okay, we have a lot to do today, but first, let's get the luggage back up to our bedroom."

"What do we do with his stuff?" Mae asked.

She thought the right thing to do would be to keep the items that were in the suitcase, but they smelled like him and the shirts they could use would make them look like him. Reminding herself and the girls of a past she didn't want them to think about was not part of her plan. "We'll put it in the garage for now."

While Mae struggled to bring her and her sister's suitcases upstairs, Sloane carted Brady's suitcase into the garage after having made sure the coast was clear. She held the woven gray carry-on suitcase aloft from the cement flooring, looking at it and knowing that the contents were all that was left of him. She let go of it and dropped it to the floor to land on its own. She turned and closed the door behind her.

The muck the sea let in, still slippery on the tile flooring, nearly caused her to careen into the wall ahead of her.

Be careful, she told herself. *You're all they've got.*

"You okay, Mom?" Wren asked from above.

"Yes. I just slipped."

Despite the opened doorway, the muggy air was already warm and caused her to sweat as she picked up her own suitcase and climbed the stairs. Wren had already laid out their cold breakfast onto the makeshift table. Today's meager meal consisted of granola with reconstituted milk poured over top. Sloane told herself this would be their first meeting of the McKenna girls. She'd make the changing of her last name back to Finn's legal as soon as possible, when humanity was up and running again, and silently vowed to never alter her name again.

After she placed her suitcase into her room, she picked up her paper bowl full of breakfast and dug in with her plastic spoon. Between bites she said, "The first thing we have to do today is dive into Trent Carson's basement to retrieve any weapons and ammunition that may be left." She motioned across the street with her plastic spoon.

"Isn't that stealing?" Mae asked her.

"No sweetheart; he asked us to do it. In fact, we are going to take care of the houses for the Carsons, the Millers, and the Bakers until they return."

"How are we going to get into their basement?" Wren asked. "It's full of water, just like ours is."

Wren was the quieter of the two girls. She internalized a lot, and Sloane suspected Wren might realize what really happened to Brady last night, whereas Mae probably thought he merely disappeared into thin air. *Poof, bye-bye, see ya*, as she liked to say.

"We can't wait for the water to recede. I'm going to have to dive for it. They probably filled their bathtubs full of water, like we did, to save fresh water before the flooding took place. We'll have to rinse any wet ammo and guns we find with the fresh water right away to get rid of the corrosive salt water. Then we'll have to dry it all out and lubricate the weapons. That's our first priority." She took another bite of granola and pointed toward the opened back door. "That's our second priority," she said when she was through crunching.

"We have to board up the back door?" Mae asked.

"Yes. We have to secure the house as quickly as possible. Then we have to figure out a way to drain these basements."

"Not just ours?" Wren asked.

"Not just ours. If we leave them filled with this seawater, the walls will start to mold throughout the houses. We have to get them dry. All of them."

"Why are we doing this for them?" Mae asked and, as she expected, Wren shot her a knowing look.

She smiled at both girls. "Because that's what good neighbors do. They help each other. We will also need to secure their homes and make sure no one breaks in while we're not watching."

"Sounds like a lot of work," Mae complained.

"It will be, but we can do it. If we make it look like those houses are occupied, no one will suspect we're here alone and vulnerable. Do you see?"

They both nodded.

"It'll be like a game," Mae said.

"Exactly, it's like a game" she said, finishing the last bite of breakfast in her bowl.

"Okay. So here are some rules we need to live by. Number one, you two don't go anywhere alone. You have to stay together. If I'm diving into the basement, you don't go wandering down the road. We're a team. Wherever I am, you need to be. If I have to leave you here, you stay together—always. Understand?"

"Yes, Mom," they both answered with their own trademark flair of sarcasm.

"I'm serious. This isn't a joke. Got it?" she chastised them.

"Yes Mom; we've been through this before. Don't worry, we understand," Wren said.

"All right. I will always keep the pistol with me, but I need to teach you girls how to shoot too; you're old enough. I'm not sure what kind of weapons Trent has down there, but we'll make do with what he has."

"I don't want to shoot a gun, Mom," Mae said, her face confused.

"We all have to learn to defend ourselves, Mae. You're thirteen. You're old enough to learn. Guns are dangerous weapons, but they will also save your life or the life of your sister."

Her younger daughter still looked perplexed by the notion but seemed to accept the explanation.

"Okay, let's get going. We'll lock up here and sneak over to the Carsons' to begin our work. Wren, you'll keep watch while I get whatever I can from the basement. Mae, you'll put what I find into the first filled tub of water. This may be the only safe water we have for a while, so we'll use just one of the tubs to clean with for now."

3

Diving the Depths

SHE COULDN'T GUARANTEE THEY WOULD GO UNSEEN IF THEY sneaked to Trent's house, so she thought the next best thing was to casually walk up to the door like normal, as if Harper herself stood within her doorway, beckoning them inside like she used to do when they visited. Trying to keep up the illusion that someone was, in fact, home in these houses was a problem she wasn't sure how to solve yet, but if they were to survive, she must.

The other houses that lined the street provided easy vantage points to see her every move, and she had no idea who remained home or which houses were abandoned. Since experiencing the chaos of the pandemic and its aftermath, people were a lot less trusting than they used to be—and with good reason. She assumed the first issue for the unprepared would be to rip off abandoned houses for their food stores. She planned to make that a problem for them in any way she could.

As luck would have it, after the pandemic passed, she had

armed herself and stocked her own home with preparedness items. They wouldn't starve, so that wasn't an immediate danger for her and the girls; however, her neighbors would come back someday and she wanted them to be as thankful as she was right now for saving her and the girls from Brady.

They stood in the foyer of their home, each one with a key to the house on a lanyard around their necks.

"Okay, this is how we're going to do this from now on," she said to the girls, hoping they wouldn't think she was out of her mind. "We have to imagine that all the neighbors are watching; we need them to believe that these houses are occupied, so we're going to pretend we're talking to them as we approach."

They both looked at her like she was nuts.

"Seriously?" Wren asked her.

"Yes. We're going to smile and wave as if Harper is standing in her doorway, waving back."

Mae looked from her to Wren, confused.

"What? We're going to walk across the street," Mae held up her hand, plastered a fake smile onto her face, waved like a princess atop a parade float, and said, *"Hi Harper, I'll be right there.*' Are you kidding me? That'll look nuts."

"Then we'll look nuts. That's what we have to do to make it look like they're home. We'll also leave flashlights on in different rooms, move stuff around, and stage the garage door open at different times of the day, as if they were home."

"Well, that's only going to be a problem for the Carsons' and the Bakers' houses. We can sneak around the back to the Millers' house to do the same, since they're next door. It won't be so bad, Mae," Wren explained.

"I'm not doing it," Mae protested and crossed her arms over her chest.

"Then you just walk along with us and stare straight ahead," Sloane said.

She opened the front door and peered outside. A wave of

steamy air hit her in the face. She knew it was muggy inside, but the outside air was just as bad—if not worse. It was going to be a long, hot summer. After checking to see if the coast was clear, she stepped outside and the girls followed her. She reminded herself to lose the frightened surveillance look in favor of smiling broadly and waving to the stagnant Carson home. She glanced behind her to see an embarrassed Mae looking anywhere but in front of her. Then there was Wren, who raised her brown eyebrows while moving her hand back and forth, doing a poor impersonation of a friendly neighbor coming over to greet them.

Sloane continued stoically, determined to pull this off. The only thing out of place in the scene was Sloane had her Glock strapped to her thigh. Even still, she was certain that in light of the current circumstances it was actually acceptable—if not a requirement—to be armed these days.

"Good morning, Harper. Thank you for having us over," she said loudly as they approached the porch.

"That's a little over the top, Mom," Mae complained in an embarrassed whisper.

"We do what we have to do," Sloane whispered out of the corner of her mouth.

She looked around behind her to see if anyone was watching them from the opposing houses. She tried the door handle. It was locked. Then she remembered Trent said he'd leave the shotgun in the garage for her to retrieve and the back sliders were all blown out anyway.

"Great plan, Mom. How are we supposed to get in with the doors locked?" Mae said.

"Follow me; we're going around back. Stay close," she said. *So much for deception. I hope the neighbors don't see us.*

They walked quickly between the houses and Sloane motioned for the girls to stick to the side of the house while she looked to see if the coast was clear. She peeked around, and other than the expected debris from the disaster strewn all over the backyard, everything was as it should be. Even part of a drape hung over their blown-out sliding glass door.

"It's open, Harper. I've got it. Thanks," she said at a normal tone, still pretending.

Both girls looked at her like she was a loon and couldn't believe their mom was still trying to keep up the charade. She walked over to the opening and waved to the girls to come along.

"Get in," she said. They stepped carefully over the littered flooring and into the living room of the Carsons' house. Not knowing what she might find inside, Sloane pulled her weapon, keeping her finger along the slide.

"Garage first," she said. They went as carefully and soundlessly as possible from the living room to the mudroom, which led to the garage.

"Ahg! It smells in here," Mae complained, pinching her nose.

"It's the trash. That and probably the stuff rotting in their deep freezer," Wren said.

"We're not going to worry about that yet. Look around for the shotgun."

"It's right there on the workbench, Mom," Wren said.

Sloane went to retrieve the gun and found a swimmer's mask with snorkel, as well as a note from the Carsons that read,

Dear Sloane,

Remember, you are welcome to anything you can salvage. Take care, Harper and Trent.

She stuffed the note into her jeans pocket and then leaned the shotgun out, tilted it to the side, and opened the action to see if it was loaded. There was a round in the chamber, and the tube magazine was loaded, although she didn't know if it was full. She knew Brady hadn't fired it, but she wasn't sure if Trent had left her with the ammo or taken it for himself; she wouldn't have blamed him if he did.

"I feel like we're breaking into their house, Mom. Are you sure about this?" Mae said.

"Me too. This doesn't feel right," Wren agreed.

"Look. It's okay. I promise you. You saw me talking to Mr. Carson outside last night, right?"

They nodded.

"We agreed to work it this way. He said we were welcome to anything we could salvage, and I promised him we'd look after his house while they were away. We made a deal and that's like a promise. I keep my promises," she said, smiling as she swiped Mae's too long bangs out of her eyes and to the side of her already sweaty forehead.

"So let's get started," she said and handed the shotgun to Wren to carry. She picked up the snorkel and mask and heard something metallic hit the concrete floor. When she looked down, she saw a set of keys on a ring. She knew immediately what they were for and was thankful that the Carsons remembered to leave them for her, or she'd have a very hard time getting into the locked storage room. She put them into her jeans pocket along with the note.

After putting the snorkel and mask into her cinch bag, she held her hand on the pistol grip of her weapon and turned from the garage back to the mudroom. Even though they came in directly across the living room and kitchen to the garage without running into anyone, she needed to be sure no one was hiding in the house already. She opened the door a crack and held a finger to her lips to keep the girls silent. She had no idea if someone else had already decided to break into the notorious Carson house. In fact, she figured she had one or two more days until the idea came to some of the neighbors they'd had trouble with four years ago during the pandemic.

She turned the corner into the kitchen and listened for any sounds of intruders. When nothing came, she motioned for the girls to follow and continued moving forward with her weapon drawn. Looking down, she saw that their flooring was covered in the same mucky pudding as her own. Her practical side told her the mess would be easier to remove while it was still wet, but that wasn't an immediate priority. *Take this one step at a time, Sloane*, she reminded herself.

They entered the living room and scanned the formal dining room. Although there were several expected footprints, each seemed to be at the same state of dull dryness—a clear indication that no one had entered the residence since the Carsons left.

"Let's check upstairs," she whispered. After they cautiously walked up the stairs, they checked the first room on the left. There were two twin beds alongside opposite walls; one was neatly made with the dusty-blue covers pulled down and tucked under the mattress, while the other remained unmade in a hasty morning retreat.

"This is Chris's room," Wren said. "It's weird. We've known them so long but I've never seen his room before."

Sloane looked at her daughter, who was a few years younger than Trent's son. "Well, that's a good thing. He was off at college. I'm sure they planned to track him."

They continued on to what both girls knew was Amy's room, their mutual friend. The girls had played over at the Carsons' on various occasions, swapping Barbie clothes when they were younger. More recently, they spent their time giggling over boys, listening to music, or complaining about their mothers.

"Amy's room," Sloane said.

"I really feel like we're intruding here, Mom," Wren said.

"I know, dear; it's not natural to be here without the Carsons, but think of it as caretaking. We're the caretakers now. We'll keep it safe for them until they return."

"Okay," Wren said as they walked into the master suite.

Sloane felt her friend Harper's presence the most there; the room still smelled of her. She walked through and peered into the master closet without going in. *No need to look.* She knew Trent would have already taken the guns he kept in there. They continued to the en suite bathroom, where they saw the tub and twin sinks filled with water. "Good. They filled them too, like we did."

On their way out of the room, they stopped by the office and the kids' bathroom. As with the other bathroom, the double sinks and bathtub held clean water. Sloane grabbed a towel from the linen closet, knowing she'd need it for her swim in the basement.

"Mae, when you bring up the ammo, I want you to put it in this tub, but don't open them, okay?"

Mae nodded.

"Okay, I think we're done," Sloane said.

"You forgot the attic, Mom," Mae said.

"Oh, that's right," Sloane replied.

She found the narrow stairs leading up to the attic-turned-video-game room. They cautiously climbed the steps, and as Sloane poked her head up into the room, she saw movement in her peripheral vision.

"Oh my God!" she nearly screamed.

"Mom?" Wren yelled, almost dropping the shotgun.

With quickened breath and her hand over her pounding heart, she looked down at the girls.

"It's... it's just a cat. It must have come through the open back door. It's okay. Let's leave it alone; we'll shoo it out later," she said.

Finding nothing other than the stray cat, they descended the stairs back to the first floor. They kept their voices at a little more than a whisper, confident no one was inside the house.

"Okay, next step. Wren, I need you to stand watch right here by the basement door. No one can see you from the front here. If you see or hear anyone, you need to walk into the basement stairwell and close the door quietly behind you. Keep the shotgun with you. Then have Mae signal me immediately.

"Mae, I'm going to reach the gun cabinet. I know where it is because that's where Trent and Harper taught me how to clean my gun. The rounds are usually in green army canisters. They're heavy. When I bring them up, you check with Wren to be sure the coast is clear and then quietly bring the first load up and submerge the whole can into the kids' bathtub full of clean water. Understand?"

"How are you going to dive into that water, Mom?" Mae asked. "It's dark and cold down there, with all kinds of stuff in it."

Sloane placed her hands on her hips and put on a brave face. "I'm a good swimmer. I can do it. You don't need to worry about me; that's my job. Give me a second while I change into my suit, and we'll get started."

Sloane stepped into the darkened basement stairwell. A musty, putrid smell hit her right away. It reminded her of the time she forgot their soaking wet beach towels in the trunk of her old Volvo over a hot weekend—only a hundred times worse. The smell made her gag. She opened the cinch bag, pulled out the flashlight, and turned it on. She shined it onto the blue-gray water level below and shivered at the thought of submersing herself into that murky seawater. *Yeah, I want to dive right into that—not! Shake it off, Sloane; you can do this,* she told herself. The water level was a few inches from the unfinished ceiling. *At least there's air for the snorkel.*

She undressed quickly and stuffed her clothing into the bag. She placed the keys into the secure left side of her swimsuit and her gun in the holster next to her boots, within quick reach if the need arose.

"Okay Mae. Come here, please," she said.

"See anything?" she asked Wren.

"No Mom. Coast is clear," Wren said.

"Remember, keep it quiet. No running up and down the stairs."

Both girls nodded.

"The sooner we get this done, the better. This house creeps me out without the Carsons," Wren said.

Sloane nodded; she felt the same way.

"You stand right here against the wall and hold the flashlight in this direction." Sloane shined it to the left of the room, hoping there would be enough ambient light to see through the water. To get to Trent's gun stash/food storage room, Sloane would have to go around a left corner at the bottom of the stairs and move forward to the end of the far wall. The light wouldn't reach the entire way, so she would have to feel her way around from memory.

"If there's an emergency, turn off the light. I'll know right away and I'll will come back quickly."

At thirteen years old, Mae wasn't a baby, but when Sloane looked into her scared face, she only saw a frightened little girl. "It's going to be fine, Mae. Let's hurry and get this over with."

Expecting the first few steps to be slippery on the unfinished, slime-water-coated stairs, Sloane held onto the stair railing as she descended into the liquid.

"Is it cold?" Mae asked.

"Just a little."

She cleared a path with her foot, moving the debris that had settled by the entrance. The water wasn't freezing, but she couldn't shake the feeling she was stepping into nothing more than sewage. Once she was waist deep, she had to say goodbye to Mae. She adjusted the mask and snorkel, smiled, and waved.

Other than keeping the nasty water out of her eyes, the goggles were worthless. The water was so dirty it left her with nearly zero visibility. And given the filthy water, Sloan pressed her lips so tight she nearly bit them together to keep the water out.

She used the unfinished wall studs as a guide, pushing herself with little thrusts along the way and recounting from memory where the room should be. She had to leave the wall several times because of floating rubbish. Her foot brushed against something soft and, for a moment, she thought it might be a body but then remembered they had a couch down there somewhere in that approximate position. She imagined things that were once held down by gravity had floated along and readjusted themselves to their own liking.

Finally, she reached the end of the studded wall, which was the corner of the room where she knew the locked storage room door stood. She felt down with her leg and knocked her shin into the doorknob. *Great!* She slipped the keys out of their position and remembered there was one for the deadbolt and one for the doorknob. One of the keys had electrical tape over the head. *I have no idea what that might mean,* she thought. First, she tried it on the doorknob lock. When that didn't work, she tried the deadbolt, which it slid into easily. *Perfect!* She finished unlocking the door with the other key. *Mystery solved.*

She tried to pull the door open; it didn't budge, so she braced one knee to the wall and pulled steadily. The door opened enough for her to get through, and suddenly, there was light pouring in through the basement window wells. While she returned the door keys securely to the thigh material of her suit, she imagined there was thick sludge settled along the floor, blocking the door's path

She knew by memory that the black metal gun case was located next to the entrance on the left. She reached her hand above the unfinished ceiling into the rafters, where she knew Trent had hidden the gun case keys and pulled them off the little nail he kept them on, hoping to hell they'd not fallen when the flood waters raced in. She remembered thinking at the time that Trent was a little nutty to keep secret keys stashed everywhere. Now, she was thankful she knew where they were.

With anticipation of what she might find inside, she opened the case door. Even though it was lighter in this room, she had to feel around for anything of value to take. On the top shelf, she felt the weight of some kind of small ammo box, the thin cardboard already disintegrating in her hand. She pulled it out and then realized she had nothing to carry any of the loose items she might find. She turned her head and spotted a bright orange Home Depot bucket bobbing in the water near the surface between the rafters. There was no way to empty it of water in the air space available so she grabbed the edge underwater and turned it upright, freeing the air trapped inside. She then lowered the small cardboard ammo box inside the bucket while she looped the wire handle over her left forearm like an underwater shopping basket.

She swept her hand along the next shelf and when it touched something that felt like metal, she recoiled automatically. She mentally shook herself and reached for it again. It was some kind of pistol, though she had no idea what make and model. She lifted it over the opened bucket and dropped it gently inside. It landed with a soft *thunk* when it met the plastic bottom.

She swept her hand through the larger cavity of the case again; on one end, she felt the barrel end of a rifle. It leaned forward when Sloane tugged it free and she lifted the whole thing away easily with the water's buoyancy. After transferring the barrel end to her left hand along with the bucket over her arm, she again felt around.

Even though this was already a treasure trove, she was hoping for more. When using her right arm to feel lower in the case turned up nothing, she gave up and instead used her right foot. When she reached the bottom there was, in fact, something else. It felt like a sealed ammo canister with a loose handle that had collapsed; she slipped her toes under the handle and was surprised at the heavy weight when she lifted it up for her hand to reach.

She slipped the ammo can into the bucket with the other finds, adding a significant amount of weight to her arm. She pulled the bucket and rifle close to her side, retrieved the keys with her right hand, and then, instead of locking an empty gun case, she reached up and looped the key ring around the nail in the rafter again.

Something touched her right arm and then the top of her head as she was leaving the key on the nail. She brushed whatever it was away behind her, barely seeing above the water level.

It touched her again and Sloane turned with a start to see

blackish brown serpent scales slithering into the water right behind her back. She panicked and screamed through the snorkel, sending bubbles rapidly through the water, and swam to the exit. The rifle and heavy orange bucket delayed her efforts, but she knew she couldn't lose them, not even in terror. As she passed through the doorway and attempted to close the door, she saw the snake slithering toward her. She pulled the awkward load out of the way quickly and pushed the door closed. She wasn't certain if the snake remained on the other side, but she told herself that it did. Even though she shook from fear, she again pulled out the double key ring and locked both the deadbolt and doorknob again. When she turned toward the stairs, her stomach knotted. The light that Mae was supposed to be holding as she stood vigil was out.

4

A Surprise

No, no, no... Sloane hastily made her way to the stairwell and surfaced out of the water. Mae was nowhere. *Please no!*

She crept up the slimy wooden stairs, hauling the bucket up to stow nearby in the dark interior. She tried to limit the splashing of the water, but she was panicking now and couldn't avoid it. She laid the rifle across the water-filled bucket. Where Mae should have been standing, Sloane instead found the turned-off flashlight. She turned it on and listened for any sounds to detect where the girls might be but only heard silence. She flashed the light onto the pile of her clothing on the ground.

Her Glock still remained inside her holster atop the pile. She grabbed the towel, dried her hands, and snatched the gun out of its strap. She crept up the stairs; as the light filtered in a line under the door, a shadow passed by, and she stopped in her tracks.

"Wren?" she finally whispered. The door opened.

"Hi Mom."

"Is everything okay? Where's Mae?"

"She's right here, *with* Nicole," Wren said in a tone trying to convey the situation at hand without saying it out loud.

"Nicole?" Suddenly Sloane went from fright back to worry. "Is... her dad here, too?" she asked in a light tone.

"No. Only Nicole," Wren said.

She loved eleven-year-old Nicole, who came to visit many times over the years since the pandemic, but her father was another story.

With the exception of his daughter Nicole, who was only five at the time, Doug had lost his entire family to the pandemic. Doug was never prepared for the deadly disease; in fact, they lived paycheck to paycheck then, never saving or preparing for a rainy day. He'd once broken into her house to steal her food while she and the girls were away and had also tried to break into Larry's house while they were home. If it weren't for Trent Carson, he would have succeeded. He'd also played a part in Trent's near death, causing everyone who made it through the crisis to keep their distance from Doug's house. After the pandemic, Doug and his daughter remained in the same house at the end of Horseshoe Lane. That left poor Nicole to grow up on her own, cast out from most of the neighborhood kids.

Over the years, Doug grew mentally unstable and obese. He was prone to outbursts aimed toward his daughter and seldom left home. He hoarded food and supplies so much that his garage was packed to the gills, quite visible to passersby whenever he'd left it opened. His truck remained in the driveway, abandoned to the elements. The house fell into disrepair and little Nicole grew quiet, rail thin, unkempt, and often wandered the neighborhood in search of kindness. It was a heartbreaking transformation she and the other neighbors witnessed over the years. Everyone helped out where they could, but Doug wouldn't allow help from any of them where Nicole was concerned.

She slipped the gun behind her and approached the landing.

Nicole and Mae sat on the stairs leading to the second floor, talking quietly and petting the stray cat that had scared her to death earlier. Noting mentally, Sloane thought it was best not to tell them about the snake in the basement.

"Hi Nicole," Sloane said. This was not good. She must have wandered over here because either her father sent her or the girls were making too much noise and she sought them out.

"Hi Sloane," Nicole said while petting the cat. Sloane saw curiosity in the child's eyes when they swept over Sloane's wet swimsuit and hand behind her back.

"What are you doing down there?" Nicole asked.

Sloane noticed something alarming about Nicole, as well; her face, though dirty from the lack of proper washing, was bruised on the left side and her lip was split. She deflected the question. "Honey, what happened to your face?" she said with concern.

Her expression immediately took on a blank stare as she lifted her hand from the cat's fur. "Ah, nothing. I fell on the slippery stairs."

Okay, that might have happened but I doubt it. I'll kill him if he's now beating her, too. Now I have to convince her that the Carsons are home with me swimming in their basement. How do I do that?

"Well, please be more careful, Nicole. There's not a lot of doctors around. Listen, the Carsons are going to be home later tonight and we needed to get our spare keys to our shed out of their basement. They told us to go ahead and get them on our own." She pulled the keys from her suit and jingled them in front of the girl.

Both of her daughters had gone stone quiet with widened eyes as their mother spun the tale. She hated to lie, but she needed to maintain the deception so Doug wouldn't find out about the empty houses.

"Oh, I thought they were gone. The Bakers are gone, too," Nicole said.

"Actually, I saw Mr. Baker checking the mailbox this morning.

They're home," Wren interjected, cutting her eyes at her mother at the end of her lie.

"Amy, too. She came over early this morning for her phone that she'd left at our house," Mae said.

Sloane thought that was perhaps going over the line a little too far. *Great. Now I've turned my children into liars as well.* It was the beginning of a life of survival and she knew she'd have to give up on many of the ethics she'd instilled in them when life was normal.

Nicole looked a little confused. "Oh, it was so quiet this morning. I thought they'd all left. A lot of people have left the neighborhood."

"Well, we're here and so are the Carsons, the Bakers, and the Millers." She said it specifically that way in case her father questioned the girl.

Nicole stood up and brushed off her shorts.

Sloane was aghast at the girl's condition. When she stood, she saw the outline of her ribs through her muddied purple t-shirt. Her legs reminded her of those horrid, emaciated teen models: too thin and scrawny.

"Nicole, have you eaten *anything* today?" Sloane had to ask the question.

She visibly swallowed.

Sloane watched as her neck muscles flexed. "Dad says we only get one meal a day now. He doesn't want to run out."

Sloane absorbed this piece of news and nodded because the last time she saw Doug, he definitely wasn't missing any meals. This left Sloane in a difficult situation. She couldn't tell the girl to come around later and have dinner. Nicole would likely tell her father, which, in their past experience, ensured a nighttime break-in. *No, she couldn't do that and endanger them all.* It was a problem—one she didn't have an answer to. For now, she'd have to let Nicole go and keep an eye on her condition as the days went on.

"Well, why don't you take that kitty along and bring him

outside, Nicole. We'll lock up the house for the Carsons and get back to our own place. Mr. Baker said he wanted to take a look at our gas lines later, so we should get back to the house," she continued the ruse.

Nicole walked out the front door with the heavy cat limp over her arm and waved goodbye. Nicole even struggled with the weight of the cat in her arms.

"Bye Nicole. See you around," the girls called after her.

"Quickly, lock the door," Sloane whispered to Wren. "How did this happen? How did she get in?" she asked them.

Wren began to explain, "Mom, I was watching the front door and then all of a sudden I turned around and there was Nicole, standing in the kitchen. She came through the busted-out back door. She scared me to death, but there was nothing I could do. I called down for Mae to come up and visit with her until you were done because I didn't want to tell her to leave so she could run off and tell her dad that we were here."

"Okay, well, let's hurry up and get out of here. Give me a second to change. I'll be right back," Sloane said and went back into the stairwell. She set the rifle aside and drained the water from the bucket as much as possible. It was very heavy now with the ammo cartridge inside, along with the pistol and waterlogged ammo box. Then she quickly dried off and redressed. Lugging the bucket and rifle through water was much easier. She wasn't sure how she was going to disguise this heavy load as they walked across the street. She now viewed boarding up the Carsons' back door as more a priority than her own, knowing that Doug would certainly take advantage of the food cache he had down there. They'd have to think of something quick.

She resurfaced from the basement dressed and burdened with the bulky items.

"So we're just going to walk across the street with that waving like lunatics?" Mae said.

"I don't see us having much choice. Instead of hiding it, we'll pretend that's why we came over—to get the guns and the bucket of stuff. If we're seen with the weapons, people will think twice about bothering us, and if we make it seem like we got them from the Carsons, they'll know the people living here are armed too because they didn't need these. Get it?"

Both girls nodded that they did.

"So we're lying our heads off so no one will think we're alone. Got it," Mae said.

Sloane wasn't sure if she really did or if that was her sarcasm working overtime.

"Are we going to rinse those here, like you said earlier?" Wren asked, pointing to the stash.

"No, we're going to do it at home. We'd better get out of here before we attract any more attention."

After locking the doors that could be locked, they stepped back through the busted opening, and Sloane wondered if Nicole came in looking for food. It wasn't like the girl to sneak into people's backyards, especially the Carsons' backyard. Hunger had a way of making you do things you normally wouldn't.

As they approached the street, Nicole was nowhere in sight but the cat was. The cat made a beeline from one end of the neighborhood to the other with a black, shaggy dog on its tail. The prey zigged and zagged back and forth, trying to lose its hunter.

"Oh Mom! We have to do something!" Wren gasped.

Sloane spoke low. "No. There's nothing we can do for it. Don't look. Come on, let's go," she said and waved back at the Carsons' house. "Thank you, Trent. We'll see you soon. Have Amy come over later."

5

Trickery

ONCE INSIDE THE HOUSE, SLOANE QUICKLY CHECKED THE windows on the second floor to observe the neighbors. She didn't hear the cat anymore and could only imagine the dog caught his lunch.

Hungry dogs. That will be a problem in the days to come.

No one else was visible up or down the road. She eyed Doug's ramshackle house for any sign of Nicole at the far end but saw none. She worried for the girl, but there was little she could do for her now.

"Should we put this stuff in our own tub?" Mae asked.

"Yes, but first, Wren, come here," she said and opened the windows of her room to let out the stifling air. "One of us must always keep watch while the others work. You scan these windows for anyone or anything. That's your job. You're my eyes. You're our sentry. You can walk from room to room, but let me know if anything moves."

"Okay Mom, I've got it," Wren said.

"All right, Mae. Let's get this stuff rinsed off and dried."

They took the rifle and submerged it in the girls' bathroom tub to rinse out the saltwater. Then they carefully pulled out the ammo canister and the pistol and submerged them, as well. Finally, Sloane pulled up the sodden cardboard ammo box that remained at the bottom and easily peeled off the top layer. She dragged out the plastic cartridge that held copper rounds all in neat rows. The smeared writing on the box said the rounds were .45 ACP. She hoped they went to the pistol at the bottom of the tub. She also hoped the ammo in the box went to the larger, gnarly looking rifle.

"What's in that heavy box, Mom?" Mae asked.

"I don't know. Let's get some towels down and find out."

They laid out a layer of dry towels on the tiled floor next to the tub and then Sloane called out to Wren with just the right tone to carry without shouting. "Status, Wren?"

"A crow landed in the street and picked up something but other than that it's all clear."

"Good, that's what I want to hear."

She and Mae sat on the floor, lifted the sealed ammo box out of the water, and placed it on the towels. They both picked up the ends of the towel and dried every crevice of the box until it went from shiny, wet, army green metal to a dull metallic. Sloane opened the latch and inside lay a jumble of large, pointy rounds.

"I'm assuming these go to that big gun," Mae said.

"Yeah... you and me both. We have to make sure they're completely dry," Sloane said. She recognized the rifle as an AR-10 and now understood why Trent might have opted to leave it behind. Due to the rifle's weight and the larger rounds, they were probably too cumbersome to carry around when he had lighter options at hand.

She ensured her fingers were free of all moisture and reached into the box and down to the bottom. Not one drop of water appeared inside.

"Whew, I think we're in luck. The seal held up. That's great news."

"Mom," Wren called, short and direct.

Sloane hopped up from her knees to standing. She peered around the corner to see Wren standing back from the window, scared as she pointed out.

"What is it?" Sloane whispered.

Her daughter waved her over, too afraid to speak. It was something she wanted Sloane to see for herself.

She sidled over to the window frame and as she looked out, she saw what had alarmed her daughter. It was Doug, standing at the foot of the Carsons' driveway, and he had obviously dragged Nicole behind him by her thin arm as well. By the distressed look on Nicole's face, he was hurting her arm in his beefy grasp and she wasn't there of her own free will.

That bastard!

She took out her Glock, her finger held with an itch along the slide.

"Mom, no. You might hit Nicole," Wren warned.

"I'm not going to hit either of them," Sloane said and aimed ten feet to the right of their position. She'd meant to scare him away, but before she began to squeeze the trigger back, the cat-eating dog appeared to their left and growled ferociously at the pair. Nicole screamed. Doug began to yell at the beast as it continued to approach them with its ominous growl.

"Mom, do something! I don't want it to get Nicole," Wren begged.

There wasn't enough time at that moment to shake her head in frustration, let alone stop it. Suddenly, the dog lunged at Doug and Nicole broke free of his grasp. She ran home while Doug's shrill voice screamed in pain as the dog's sharp teeth embedded into the man's thigh.

The panicked man kicked at the dog with his other leg in an attempt to pry him loose. All the while, his arms flailed about and his dirty green, ripped t-shirt rode up over his swollen belly, exposing him for the gluttonous pig he'd become.

"Should we do something?" Mae asked from behind them.

"I don't know," Sloane said.

This dog is doing us a favor.

"I've got an idea! Wren, keep watch and if the dog or Doug attacks me, I want you to shoot the shotgun into the air. Straight out into the open. Mae, stay here with your sister."

"Mom, where are you going?" Wren said.

She stopped at her closet and ripped a belt off a hook in the doorway then smiled and said, "I'm going to go feed the dog."

She raced down to the kitchen, being careful to not slide again and break her neck in the slime. She opened the refrigerator and, once past the putrid wave of spoiled food, she grabbed the casserole covered in plastic wrap that she had thawed the night before the tidal wave hit. Doug's high-pitched screaming still echoed through the house, so she knew the attack was still going on. She took out her weapon, unlocked the front door, and stepped out. After closing the door behind her, she walked to the end of the drive with the casserole in one hand and her Glock in the other.

Doug didn't even register her approach. She stopped, sat the casserole on the concrete driveway, and dug her free hand into the dish. She scooped out a room temperature, smelly mass of hamburger and cheese tater tots then stood and pierced the air with her best whistle. The dog responded first. It growled at her, still clenched to its victim's thigh. She tossed the treat five feet in front of it.

She hoped the dog would go for it. It certainly was much more appetizing than Doug's sweaty, bloated thigh was on any given day. The appealing smell must have hit the dog because as Doug kicked it again, it released him and went to investigate the splattered mass on the road. Doug began to jog away while Sloane tossed another handful closer to herself as the dog finished the last pile. She talked sweetly to the animal. "That's right. Here's the food."

Doug stopped another fifteen feet away and said, "Thank you, Sloane." He waved his bloodied hand at her.

She glared at him. "Stay away from here, Doug, or Trent will kill you."

He sneered at her. "They left. Trent isn't home."

I need him to doubt those words.

"Yes, he is. His gun's trained on you even now."

Doug quickly glanced at the Carson house.

"Why do you think I feel safe out here with you now? We're always watching you, Doug. We won't ever forget what you're capable of."

He looked scared shitless, and she couldn't resist adding, "And if you lay another hand on Nicole, I'll see you dead. I'll kill you myself." The words she spoke made her tremble inside. Hurting a child was the lowest thing man was capable of.

He sneered at her and turned away, walking back toward his own wretched house.

She watched him go while she doled out more food to her new best friend.

"We don't like him, do we?" she cooed to the dog. "But I'm sure this is much better food for you, buddy."

After Doug had returned to his abode, she continued to lure the dog closer to her while constantly giving words of encouragement.

A little at a time, the large, black, shaggy dog went from ferocious to seeming desperately hungry. It was close enough now to see a collar around its neck with the typical engraved metal tags. This animal was someone's pet.

She took the belt out and looped one end through the buckle. This time she attempted to feed the animal out of her hand, reaching the globby mess out to him. "Gentle, please," she said, hoping he wouldn't take her fingers off with the food.

He was tentative in his approach but he licked at her fingers and then ate it right out of her hand. She moved her hand away and this time put another handful through the loop in the belt, leaving a wide opening, and then did it again.

"Good boy," she said as he began to chew the contents out of her hand again.

Carefully, she lifted the loop evenly from her own arm and over the dog's head. She didn't cinch it yet; she held it loose and again offered more food. Slowly, she began closing the loop around the dog's neck while he was busy devouring the decayed casserole, until she had enough length to wrap the belt around her left hand twice to ensure she had a handle on the dog. She picked up the casserole pan, now half-empty, and began to guide the animal toward the Carsons' house.

Making plans on the fly, she realized this dog was security. Doug was terrified of it and he wouldn't approach the Carsons' house if he heard the dog inside. Somehow, she needed to get this furry guy inside the house and keep it happy in there.

She was beginning to run out of tater tot casserole as she neared the backyard. She continued to talk sweetly to the dog with the hope that she could coax him inside once the food was gone. He began to lick the casserole dish and she started tugging a little harder on the belt leash as she aimed them into the opening. So far, he didn't know his stomach was leading him into a trap and she hoped to get him to the Carsons' refrigerator before he realized her aim to imprison him.

"Come on, boy. Just a little farther," she said.

Once in the kitchen and only three feet from the refrigerator, he stopped. He looked at the now licked-clean casserole pan and then at her. He lowered his head and began a low, guttural growl.

Oh shit!

She swung open the door of the refrigerator and then remembered, in horror, that the Carsons were vegetarians.

What are the chances that there's any meat in here?

"Look," she tried with a singsong voice. She pulled out what looked to be a black-eyed pea salad. She lifted the lid and the dog sniffed at the vinegar smell but didn't dive in.

Great.

Again, she reached into the darkened refrigerator and pulled out another mystery container. She lifted the lid and found what might have been a noodle casserole at one point. She offered it to the dog and he barely smelled it before taking a big mouthful.

"Good boy," she said.

Thank God!

She looked at the opened doorway and knew it was a problem she was going to have to fix before the day was through. She had to close up the opening somehow.

While the dog ate, she looked for a place to stash him temporarily while she got the house closed up. The nearest room with doors was the mudroom door leading to the garage so again she led him with the new bowl of food into the mudroom. He was under her food-driven trance again and she cooed encouragement while leading him with the bowl. Once inside, she put the bowl down, let go of the makeshift leash, and closed the outer door.

"Whew!" she said once on the other side.

Quickly, she ran back outside and across the street. Both of her girls were looking anxiously at her from the second-floor window. She waved again at the Carsons' house and said, "I'll be right back, Harper."

From their perch above, her daughters shook their heads at her like she was certifiably nuts. She was beginning to think they were right.

6

Stayin' Alive

"Quick, grab the cordless drill out of the garage."

"But there's no power, Mom," Wren said.

"It has a battery; it'll work—it's been charged."

Sloane washed her hands in the kitchen sink, hoping the running water remained uncontaminated. They wouldn't be foolish enough to test it by drinking it, but if it came down to having to use it, she had decontamination pills stowed in her supplies.

Think, dammit. What can I use to close up their blown-out door?

"Gosh Mom, you scared us. That dog was really terrifying," Mae said beside her.

She dried her hands. "That was someone's pet. He was only hungry. Now he's going to be our best asset."

"You put him in the Carsons' house?" Wren asked, returning with the cordless drill.

"Yes. He'll be a great deterrent for anyone trying to rip off the houses—especially Doug. If we come across any more stray dogs, we'll do the same thing. Okay, I know we don't have any screws long enough to go through plywood to cover the hole. Who might have long screws in their garage?"

"Maybe the Carsons do?" Wren said.

"No... Trent Carson is well known for *not* having great carpentry skills," she laughed.

"Maybe Mr. Baker does. He built the deck off the back of their house last fall," Mae said.

"Hey, you're right. Let's go check it out. Mae, grab those old peanut butter cookies and anything else that might keep the dog happy. Nothing with chocolate or pistachios though."

"Well, that's just selfish, Mom," Mae said as she rummaged through the pantry, a little surprised by her mother's attitude.

Sloane scoffed. "I'm not being selfish, Mae. Dogs can't have either of those things. They're allergic to them."

"Well, we wouldn't know about that, would we? Because you've never let us have a dog," Mae argued back.

"Ugh, now you'll have all the dogs you've ever wanted. Hurry, we're wasting time."

They carried their load and ran across the street over to the Bakers' house. The sun was now high overhead, scorching them from above and boiling them from below. The moist, radiant heat from the waterlogged earth seemed to release steam with each step they took. Staying ever vigilant, Sloane carried the Glock in one hand and led the girls across the yard. As they approached the backyard, Sloane saw something with a bluish cast lying in the grass by the far end of the property, near the corner of the house. She stopped short and turned to face the girls.

"Close your eyes."

"Why..." began Mae.

"Just do it!" she whispered forcefully. "Wren, stay behind Mae, hold onto her other arm, and follow me," she directed and pulled Mae by the forearm up the porch steps carefully so that neither girl tripped. She kept herself between the girls and the grisly scene only ten feet away.

"Agh! What is that horrible smell?" Mae said, blindly swatting at flies buzzing nearby.

"Shh, be quiet," Sloane said. She looked into Larry Baker's house and listened for any commotion. They were certainly making enough noise to make their presence known.

Once the girls were safely through the doorway, Sloane stood in the opening and said, "I don't want either of you to look out here. There's a dead body. It must have washed up from the wave."

"Oh God, the smell..." Mae complained, but Wren looked at her with sad eyes.

Sloane was afraid Wren inferred who the dead body really was. She took one last look behind her. With the moist heat of summer, the decay process was accelerated. The blue-cast skin sagged while the rest of the body bloated. She only knew who it was by the clothing he wore and the black watch around his wrist. She'd felt that watch hit her during many beatings she sustained over the years. Flies buzzed in a hover above Brady's body, feasting. She'd never hated anyone in her life. Hate required a part of your heart and she felt nothing for him now, not even human remorse.

"Let's get what we need and get out."

I'll take care of this later.

They all looked and listened for anyone or anything out of the ordinary. It had only been a few days and she speculated that most people bent on robbery would take action in one or two more days to come. She had only a little time to secure these houses but not much more than that.

They went into Larry's garage, and not only did he have building materials in there, he had boxes of large screws in stacks on his workbench.

"Look, Mom, they also have plywood sheets," Wren said.

"Yeah, but I don't think it's going to look inconspicuous hauling a sheet of plywood over to the Carsons' place, do you? And look, they're warped from the water."

"No. You're right. There must be something we can use at their own house to cover the hole," Wren said.

Sloane grabbed several boxes of the screws and handed them to the girls to carry, along with the dog's treats.

"Well, let's hurry. That dog is probably eating a hole through the door by now."

Once they returned to the Carsons', they could hear the dog whining on the other side of the door. He began barking, as well, as soon as he heard the three approaching.

"Mae, go ahead and shove a few cookies underneath the door, but don't open it."

"Okay, Mom," Mae said. Sloane then heard the girl talking to the dog in a sweet voice, trying to charm him just like she had done earlier.

With a press of the switch, Sloane tested the drill to make sure it worked and was relieved when a whirling noise answered. *I should have done that earlier.*

"Wren, look around for something we can screw to the opening. These sliding glass doors have proven to be a real pain. I want to change ours to a regular door after all of this is over."

"It's not likely we'll have another tsunami wave, Mom," Wren assured her as she went from room to room, looking for something to convert into an efficient barrier.

Sloane listened to her daughter's logic as she tested the drill bit's fit to the screws. *Perfect fit.*

"With our luck, we'll have another catastrophe in another four years. This seems to be a pattern now."

Wren took to the stairs and rummaged through the rooms for something to block the entrance with while Sloane checked the study. With once luxuriously soft leather chairs, the room was far from its best days. Wren's quick steps descended the stairs.

"There's nothing up there that will work, unless you want to use the mattresses."

"No, that won't do. There's got to be something here we can use."

"Mom," Wren said.

Sloane looked around the corner and saw her daughter standing in front of the dining room. She walked over to her as Wren pointed to the large, rectangular, formal dining table. They both looked in unison back to the sliding glass door opening and back to the table.

"Hmm. I think that'll have to do."

They began removing all the random items that were placed there in haste. "I wonder if these come off," Wren said about the table legs.

Sloane knelt down and looked underneath. "They're screwed in with hex screws; I don't have one of those. Let's drag it into the den." They each lifted one end of the table and stepped with quick baby steps to get the hefty, awkward piece of furniture past a hallway, around the kitchen, and by the den couch. Once in approximate position, they turned it on the long side and then Sloane said, "Let's lean it up now against the opening and see how it fits."

They both heaved and shoved the once valuable table against the opening where the sliding glass doors once stood. Sloane knew Harper loved this table and had bought it from the Ethan Allen furniture store in Portland, the same store where she'd purchased the leather chairs in the study. "I shudder to think how much this thing cost. Looks like it will cover most of the opening though."

"Will they be mad?" Wren asked.

"I don't think so. It's pretty much ruined, anyway. Hold it still," she said. While Wren leaned her weight against the table, Sloane began power drilling the large screws from the bottom of the tabletop and into the doorframe at one-foot intervals around the perimeter. After the table was securely in place, she and Wren stood back from their handiwork. With the four legs sticking out straight, it looked sort of like the entire house was on the wrong end.

"Well, it's not pretty, but no one's getting through there. Still, I wish we had a few two-by-fours to close up the extra space," Sloane noted.

"How about this, Mom?" Wren said, holding up one of Harper's inspirational signs from the wall. This one said, *Find Joy in the Journey.*

"Perfect. Not sure I agree with the sentiment, but it'll work for this. Are there any more of these around?" she asked while covering up the extra space on the side of the table.

"Yeah, here's one from the kitchen," Wren said.

Sloane checked the long sign; it was adorned with a depiction of many endearing farm animals and below the pictures it said, *We don't eat our friends.* She couldn't help it; she started laughing her head off.

"What's so funny? Don't judge them," Wren admonished her mother.

She wiped her eyes and shook her head. "I'm just finding joy in the journey, that's all."

"Mom!" Wren said again.

"I'm outta dog snacks," Mae called from the mudroom door. "We need something more."

Sloane quickly screwed the sign above the last one, fully enclosing the opening.

"Perfect timing then," Sloane said.

"Let me get some fresh water for him before you let him out. Wren, get something to block the stairs. Let's keep him on the main floor."

While she heard Wren pushing furniture around, she searched the cupboards for a bowl to fill with water. Again, she wasn't sure if the water from the tap was still sanitary but it looked clear and didn't seem to have a foul odor. She'd try it out on the dog first. If he suffered any ill effects, well... then she would know for sure.

"I think he's nice, Mom. He's licking my hand through the door," Mae said.

"He just wants to eat your fingers," Wren cautioned.

"Wait a minute. We need to show him we are the giver of good things. We're going to feed him and give him water and keep him happy so he'll think we are his family. We've seen he can attack, so let's remember that. Girls, get behind me," Sloane directed.

After she placed the water and more food on the tile floor in the kitchen, she pulled out the Glock again, just in case. She'd hate to kill the dog, but she also couldn't risk an injury to herself or one of the girls.

She stood by the mudroom door with her hand on the door handle.

Please let this work.

She opened the door with big smiles but held the Glock handy. "Hi buddy. Want some more food?" she said as if she were talking to a cartoon minion. The once ferocious dog panted and held a silly grin on his canine face. "I bet you want some water, too." She kept up the voice as the big black dog followed her. It stopped when it saw the girls standing behind her, and a wave of panic flooded her. Mae lowered her hand to let him sniff her. "Careful," Sloane said.

He began licking any remaining cookie residue. Wren then lowered her hand but with slow, shaky fortitude. The dog sniffed her too, and Sloane felt somewhat relieved. She walked into the kitchen, calling the dog, "Come here, boy. Come get the water."

He followed her into the kitchen and sniffed. He then began lapping up the water. She removed the trailing belt that she'd used as a leash earlier.

"Great. Now what?" Wren said.

Sloane breathed a sigh of relief. "Now we keep him on the

main floor. Let him have the run of the place. If anyone other than one of us tries to get in here, they're toast.

"We'll keep the basement door shut too and we'll feed him whatever is left in our refrigerator or freezer until it runs out or goes way too bad even for the dog. I don't want him to get sick."

He looked up at her like he was in love and she patted him. "You're my hero."

"Can I name him?" Mae asked.

"Uh, sure. Well, let's see if he already has a name." She looked at the metallic tags dangling from his collar while he tried to lick her face. Then she remembered those teeth were earlier connected to Doug's flabby thigh. "Ugh," she said, wiping off the slime. "Looks like he's from Seaside and his name is Ace." Suddenly the dog sat down on his haunches.

"Is that your name? Ace?" Mae asked.

"Ah, geez; his tail's wagging now," Wren said and patted his head.

"He's someone's lost pet. When things get back to normal, we'll try to find his owners. Don't get too attached," Sloane warned them.

Sloane walked to the mudroom and grabbed the front door keys on the hook she noticed before. "We've got to get going now. We'll come back later, let him out to go to the bathroom, and bring him more food. We'll throw a ball and play with him a little too. For now, though, we've got to work on our own house. Let's go."

He followed them to the door and once they locked up, Sloane looked through the window and Ace ran back to his food bowl. She knew it wasn't an ideal situation but it would keep the house secure for now—at least from Doug, anyway.

7

Security

SHE HAD NO IDEA THIS DAY WOULD COME WITH SO MANY distractions. She found herself continuously looking toward Nicole's house, hoping to get a reassuring glimpse of the girl.

After pulling the still submerged rifle out of the tub of water, she began drying it as well as possible. She had done the same with the pistol, which she had identified as a Colt 1911 by the engraving on the slide. Then she dumped the plastic tray of rounds onto the dry towel for Mae, whose job it was to dry each one thoroughly. Wren watched for movement again while Sloane worked.

"Hand me those cotton swabs, Mae," Sloane said.

"Do we have to get it all?" Mae asked, frustrated with the task.

"Yes, or they'll rust and then be useless to us. After this, we'll have to oil them down with my cleaning kit." Never in her life did she think she would be sitting on the bathroom floor, pulling apart and drying an AR-10 as if her and her daughters' lives depended on it. No, her dreams began a lifetime ago, when she studied in Paris and wanted nothing more than to live there. Instead, she ended up meeting Finn, falling in love, having two beautiful daughters, and teaching French at the local high school. Though she'd never change those parts of her life, she would certainly have changed Finn's death during the pandemic. So many of her dreams were now shattered and, regretfully, never to be.

"Mom, I'm hungry," Mae said.

Sloane was too; though she'd stored enough food for them for three months, she was concerned about using the surplus too quickly. *I'll have to keep an eye on that.* They were using so much more energy than they would in a normal day, she could see why the girls might be hungrier.

"We'll get something in a few minutes. Let's put these on my bed; the opened window will dry them a little more," she said. Sloane then turned to her other daughter to question, "Anything new, Wren?"

"No Mom," she answered.

Sloane decided they should use up some of the plastic encased crackers and peanut butter they'd rescued from the rising floodwaters the day before. She pulled out a few paper plates and smeared a few spoonfuls onto the little squares. *This will have to do for now.*

She glanced at her own blown out sliding glass door on the first floor. *That's got to be next. I can't sleep without securing the door.*

She brought the snacks, aboard paper plates, to both girls. Wren stood near the master bedroom window and glanced briefly at her as she placed the plate on the nightstand. Sloane again glanced toward Doug's house. "Nothing?"

"No. It's so hot, Mom. I wish we at least had a fan," Wren complained.

"Yeah, that's a problem but not a priority right now. I'll have

Mae relieve you after you eat and then you and I can cover our own door," Sloane said.

"Okay, thanks, Mom," Wren said.

Sloane skipped her own lunch only because she had too much to do. She raced downstairs to the garage and retrieved the extra battery for her electric drill. She knew once the charge was out, that was it. Without electricity, they were worthless. *Maybe Larry or Brian has one, too.* It was imperative she get her own house secure for tonight. She also knew she might be using a hammer and nails to secure the Baker and Miller homes, but that would have to do.

She looked around her own garage. *What do I use to secure my own door?* Before Finn's death, he'd intended to build another shed in the backyard. For four years, unused sheets of plywood and two-by-fours lay against one end of the garage. At some point, she ceased to see the pile; it remained there, seen only by her subconscious. The flooding waters jostled the items around, and now the wood was damp but still usable for this purpose. She worked her way past her inoperative minivan and the plastic totes full of items too young for the girls but too memorable to part with. After creating a path through what seemed like her life, she located the damp wood. *This will have to do.*

With all her might, she hauled the first soaked wooden sheet up and over the wreckage that was now worthless to them. Once free, she tilted it on its side and went back for another. It would take two sheets to cover the doorway if she overlapped them a bit. Lord knew she didn't have any nifty inspirational signs to use in her house; if she did, they'd be in French, with an intentional slight to Brady. *Les hommes pensent moins, plus ils parlent. Should have done more thinking and less talking, Brady.*

Through the opened garage door, she said, "Mae, go ahead and take over watch for your sister. Wren, come down and give me a hand."

Over the next half hour, she and her daughter drilled screws into the perimeter of her own missing sliding glass doorway. Once done, she felt a wave of relief pass over her. Now she could lock up the house securely at night. Barring a broken window, which she would hear, their home would be safeguarded.

Back to the weapons in the sweltering heat upstairs, she liberally applied the solvent that Trent previously informed her worked best. She added more to the pistol using a clean dry sock and let it soak in while she checked on the girls, who were both watching the neighborhood with bored anticipation.

"Anything new?"

"No Mom, nothing—absolutely nothing," Wren said flatly.

"That's good news, my dear. That's how we want it. We aren't prepared yet and we're racing to get prepared. Before long, there will be trouble and we need to be ready."

She wiped the solvent off after she thought the job was done, and with another clean sports sock, she rubbed until the sock came away clean instead of black. She had a whole pile of blackened sports socks but had no idea if she should burn them or wash them. She supposed she'd deal with that later.

Luckily, when Trent recommended the cleaning kit, he made sure she got the one with several bore brushes of varying sizes and a set of cleaning rods. He'd told her she never knew when she might need to clean a larger gun, and as it turned out, he was right; here she was cleaning an AR-10. She stuffed the largest bore brush she had in her kit—.30 caliber—down the bore of the rifle and pulled it out. She repeated the process over and over again and then ran a clean patch down the barrel several times to ensure it was clean and unobstructed.

Without really knowing how to lightly oil this particular rifle, she relied on what Trent had taught her: to oil all the moving parts, like the bolt and trigger assembly. She looked for areas of wear and made sure to oil those well but avoided the firing pin because he said the oil would only guarantee collection of debris in that area and cause gunk to form.

She repeated the process for the pistol and cleaned up afterwards. She made sure the rounds were fully dry and then loaded both magazines with their respective ammo. Luckily, the .308 from the ammo can was for the AR-10 and the .45ACP from the soaked cardboard box belonged to the pistol. She wanted to test them out, but that would attract attention. It would have to wait.

As the day lengthened, she still had to begin the process of draining the basements and she also had to take care of one more task before she could sleep. She dreaded the act and mentally tried to focus on the best method of performing it. Once the girls were asleep that night, she intended to sneak out, remove Brady's body from the back of Larry's house, and haul him off into the woods to rot there—out of sight and out of mind.

8

Midnight Ride

"I'm tired, Mom!" Mae whined while she stood on one leg and scratched the other with the toe of her boot.

"We're all tired. Let's get this done before the sun goes down and then we can lock up for the night." She unhooked the green lawn hose and pulled it hand over fist out of Brian Miller's yard. After handing this coiled bundle to Mae, they searched the other side of his house for any more hoses.

"I think that's it, Mom," Wren said. "We've stolen all their hoses now, so what are we going to do with them all?"

"We're going to try and drain the basements. We have ten hoses and four houses to drain, so let's put two in each house and the extras in ours." She brushed the grime from her forehead with her arm. They were all filthy and exhausted, and there was still work to do. "I have no idea how well this will do the job, but it's a start. We'll check them daily and adjust as we go. I'm sure they'll clog from the debris, but when we check on the houses, that'll be one of the chores several times a day."

At one of the Millers' broken basement window wells, Sloane knelt down and fed a hose through the window, into the seawater trapped below. "We have to feed the hose out into the water, submerging the length as we go. Try to keep it as straight as possible. Then, when you get to the end of the hose, you want to lower it into the water and point the opening up underwater to release any air. Then reach down and cup your palm over the opening so that the water is suctioned to the palm of your hand. Then let gravity do its job." She looked to where she could lay the hose out downhill. She pulled out a length of seven feet, feeling it heavy with water, and laid it where the earth sloped downhill and into the woods behind the Millers' house.

When she released her palm, the water started to drain immediately from the force of gravity and the thrust of her hand downward. "See? It's not a perfect process, but it will drain. We'll have to unclog them several times a day and restart the process, but it will work in time."

She had another cautionary thought but wasn't sure how to tell them without scaring them since being terrified of snakes was a genetic trait in their family. "By the way, watch for snakes in the basement." Both girls stepped back.

"What?" Wren said with a clip of her tongue. "Snakes? You didn't say anything about snakes earlier."

She tried to calm her daughter. "We must face our fears, no matter how scary. Just be aware there might be frogs, snakes, and anything else that could have come in with the floodwater down there. Look before you put your hand anywhere; it's better to be safe than sorry." She just could not help the motherly sayings. They came out automatically at times like these.

"That's just great, Mom." Wren said.

Her daughter shuddered as they looked around for another opening into the Millers' basement. Near the locked bulkhead door, there was a cracked window. Sloane finished it off with her boot so she could reach in and do the same thing with the next hose.

Afterwards, she said, "We'll do ours and then the Carsons' across the street; by that time, it'll be too dark to do the Bakers', so we'll wait until tomorrow to start on that one." She'd planned it this way because she didn't want the girls to get a chance at identifying the body in Larry's backyard.

They fed Ace again after placing the hoses through two cracks in the Carsons' house. They let him out to do his business and Sloane was a bit concerned the dog might make a run for it, but he returned merrily as they walked into the house. He seemed overjoyed to have his own pad. He'd made himself comfortable on Trent's former chair, proclaiming this now as his castle. The ferocious dog was now a happy, playful guy. As they said their goodbyes, they locked him in and Sloane watched as he returned to his chair in the living room, where she knew he had the perfect view over his new domain.

※

BACK AT THEIR OWN HOME, AS THE PURPLE DUSK MET THE evening sky, they quickly placed four hoses at various positions to drain their own basement. Two of the hoses, Sloane fed through to the front yard and the water ran down into the debris-strewn street. She removed several things clogging the storm drain so the water could meander down and escape into the depths under the road. The girls were becoming crankier as the evening wore on. They swatted at bloodthirsty mosquitoes and wiped at the sweaty slime now covering their skin.

"Okay, inside," she said and they locked up their home for the night. She had no idea what calamities might be happening to her neighbors on their journey and she worried about them as the sky blackened to night.

Nicole remained on her mind, too. Her physical condition worried her. Only the days to come would prove whether or not she needed to act. She felt helpless where the girl was concerned.

"Can we take showers?" Wren asked.

In an apologetic tone Sloane said, "No, but we can use the water we soaked the guns in. It's not totally sanitary, but we can towel wash. Just don't get it in your eyes or mouth. We'll work on that later, but for now, let's conserve the water we have."

A slight breeze mercifully wafted through the windows. They ate a quiet dinner of tuna mixed with red wine vinegar on yet more crackers. They were using up whatever they managed to salvage from their kitchen before Sloane opted to break into the food stores she kept in her attic. Like Trent's house, she had the nifty, finished attic. She'd chosen to put her food stores in hers when Brady had taken over the basement as his 'man cave'. He wouldn't allow her penchant for hoarding extra food and supplies down there. Instead, that was where he kept his expensive sound system and drank to his heart's content. She had hated him for taking over her home, but now she couldn't be more thankful. She had her supplies, unmolested by the floodwaters, and all of his worthless equipment was submerged underwater, along with slimy serpents of the sea. She would enjoy removing every sign of him in the coming weeks but first, she had to remove him.

Once the girls were cleaned and happily snuggled into her bed, she said, "Goodnight. I'm going to stay up for a little longer and keep watch in the den. I'll wake Wren in a few hours to take over while I sleep and then it will be your turn, Wren, to wake Mae. Don't leave the room, only watch out the window. If you hear anything, wake me."

They both agreed so quickly that Sloane feared they didn't really take her seriously. They were so tired, they'd agree to anything as long as they could close their eyes at the moment. All of them had only had a few hours of sleep over the past few days.

She didn't really blame them. Without Brady, though, their lives would be easier—even in an apocalypse, as it were.

Their snores came quickly. She mentally prepared herself for the remaining task. *I can do this. It's just a body.*

With work gloves on, a spare blanket over her shoulder, and a short piece of spare plywood in her hands, she grabbed the small flashlight and locked the side door of the garage as she left. She then made her way over to the dead body in Larry's backyard. She'd planned to haul him into the woods behind Larry's house, as far she could, to keep the decaying smell at bay.

She suspected there were more bodies out there anyway, caught by the wave. Every now and then, when the wind blew just right, she got the distinct aroma of what she knew to be decay. The smell could be an animal, but she knew there were several people who probably succumbed to the traveling wave. It happened so fast but, thankfully, it came so early in the morning that most people were still asleep instead of driving on their morning commute.

"Quick and easy," she said to herself, willing each step. "Shove the bastard on, cover him up, and haul him away."

I should probably stop talking to myself. It's a sign of insanity. It's bad enough I'm turning my daughters into liars.

As her steps neared him, her body told her not to go any closer. "God, I wish I couldn't smell him." She'd given up caring about insanity.

Gagging harder the closer she got, she said out loud, "Suck it up, buttercup."

She put the end of the flashlight into her mouth while she laid down the items she brought along. She wedged the plywood underneath his head—which, thankfully, was turned away from her. His head was stiff, but his brown hair moved and glistened with beads of moisture in the ambient light. She didn't want to see his open, bug-eaten, eyes. She began to heave as she imagined larvae swarming in there. She quickly had to remove the flashlight from her mouth while she gagged several times. "Get through this, dammit!"

She picked up the blanket, whipped it open, and covered Brady's dead body with it. "Okay, you bastard, last ride," she said and reached down with her gloved hands. She grabbed the stiff form through the blanket and around the shoulders and then hauled him onto the board, leaving several inches for a handhold near his head.

She tested out the cumbersome load, knowing it would be a difficult trip. She pulled and began to drag him, looking behind her in the dark. The chirping of crickets kept her company and the thought occurred to her that if they stopped their cadence, it would mean trouble. They were her witnesses and accomplices in this morbid crime.

Once she hit the forest, her progress slowed a bit as she maneuvered around the many trees and bushes. It took longer than she'd hoped, but when she came to a comfortable distance, she decided only ten feet more. She heaved the load again, then slipped on loose grass and fell down on her ass.

This is it, you bastard, your final resting place.

She thought about leaving the plywood sheet and blanket there but felt he didn't deserve the comfort. She pulled away the blanket and tipped over the plywood. She began to head back when she heard a noise in the nearby brush. Instantly, she pulled her Glock and flashed her light in the culprit's direction. She was getting pretty good at pulling the trigger in an instant.

It's probably Doug, dammit.

Her heart leapt into her throat as a metallic jingle preceded a dirty white puffball from beneath a bush. She'd nearly fired at the small dog that was now yipping at her legs as if she were its long lost owner.

She reached down to pet the dog, but it scampered a few feet away. "Well, be that way, but I have food where I'm going," Sloane said and picked up her gear. As she walked away, the little dog followed at a short distance.

Once she reached the garage, she tossed the items inside and coaxed the dog to follow, using a charming voice and an offer of treats. She left it in the locked, dark garage while she retrieved a box of cereal to feed him. When she returned, she flashed the light around and found the little dog curled up on the blanket she'd tossed on the ground earlier. She poured a cup of cereal near the blanket, and after the dog sniffed the food, it began to eat. "If I put you in with Ace, he'll probably eat you." She picked out several sticks from the dog's fur and petted the dog while it ate. She then noticed the little red collar about its neck and said, "Sally's your name, huh? Well, Sally, this is where you sleep tonight. Maybe we'll move you to Larry's house tomorrow. Goodnight."

When she finally washed off Brady's death from her hands, she found that the rest of her still smelled of him. He was persistent that way—never taking no for an answer, even in death. She ended up removing all of her clothes and started to wash from the top down; she shampooed her hair over the bathroom sink and then cleaned herself, from her face down to her toes, removing every last molecule she could get to.

9

New Dawn

AT THE CRACK OF DAWN THE NEXT MORNING, SLOANE CHECKED the draining hoses by herself and let the girls sleep in. She'd left the windows open upstairs so she could hear them if they spoke above a normal level. She enjoyed the cool morning breeze as it chilled her bare shoulders. Before long, the hot afternoon sun would bake them.

After she'd finished checking the Carsons', she let Ace accompany her on her morning rounds. He trotted alongside her like her own personal protector. At each house, she arranged things differently than they were before. Trent now had his lawnmower parked in the side yard and the Bakers were airing out sofa cushions on their porch. In addition to several different windows opened than the day before, the Millers also had several conspicuous, clear, plastic bags tied around the green leafy branches of the blueberry bushes lining their driveway. No one would question this about the Millers because they were known to be avid survivalist types. It was a great way to collect extra sterile water, and she was glad she had remembered seeing them do this as an experiment the summer before.

By the time she returned home, the new little dog, Sally, was yipping from the garage and letting her presence be known. She let Ace sniff at the garage door while she listened to the girls rousing upstairs.

"What's that sound, Mom?" Mae whispered loudly.

"It's a little, fluffy white dog I let in last night. Her name is Sally."

"You named her, Sally?" Mae asked.

"No. That's the name on her tag. She was someone's pet too."

She observed Ace sniffing at the doorway. He wasn't growling.

"You promise not to eat her?" He looked back at her with big, brown, soulful eyes. She opened the door, though there was a standoff for a few minutes. When little Sally yipped and lunged up to confront the larger dog, Ace only looked back up at Sloane as if to say, *What is that annoying thing?*

Then both dogs simultaneously turned, cocked their ears forward, and appeared to be alerted to something Sloane herself did not hear.

"What? What is it?" she said.

Ace went to the front door and barked, with Sally right behind him.

Then she saw the man on his bicycle. There were two more dogs with him. One was a short but long-bodied mixed breed and the other, a large yellow Labrador. Sloane's first thought was, *And so it begins... what the hell does this guy want?* It was quickly followed by her second thought of, *Great—I wonder if I can get him to leave the dogs with me?*

The bicyclist was a man in his thirties with a shoddy appearance. He was eyeing Larry's house and then Trent's while the dogs sniffed around the roadway. Sloane heard the girls on the above floor move around, and bicycle guy then scanned her house.

She had to think of something to say quickly to somehow warn them of the danger. Suddenly it came to her. She yelled in a singsong voice, "Cachez-vous" which translated directly from French as "hide yourselves". Both of her girls were taught French from an early age and would instantly understand what their mother was saying. She knew it had worked when the noise above ceased right away.

Sloane watched the bicycle guy through the window. When he reached behind his back, she thought, *I might rename him 'dead guy' here in a minute.* She went to the door and allowed him to see she was armed with the holster on her hip.

"Can I help you?" she asked him with Ace and Sally by her side.

His eyes slipped over her from top to bottom. She knew she was an attractive lady, even in her forties. She'd seen the looks over the years but never took advantage of the asset.

"I think you can," came his suggestive reply. It was the slimy way he said it—more than the words—that put him in the 'dead' column. She pictured him lying in the woods next to Brady's dead body. She hoped it didn't come to that, but there was no way bicycle guy was getting past her and to her daughters.

"Just so we understand each other, there is an AR-10 trained on you, right now, from across the street." She nodded toward the Carsons' house. "Another weapon on you from my neighbor next door." She bobbed her head to the left. "As well as the house on the right."

His eyes darted in all directions as she continued, "If you have legitimate business here, state it. Otherwise, I suggest you get back on your bicycle and leave."

Ace began a deep, guttural growl. She pretended it didn't worry her. She didn't think bicycle guy was too bright; she could almost see the rusty wheels turning as he tried to decide whether or not she was bluffing.

"I'm just looking for a place to stay," he complained.

"These houses are all occupied by their owners. I suggest you keep moving. The day is young and you're still alive—so far."

He looked from her to Ace.

The yellow lab with him had taken up a position behind him. She didn't think the dog liked Ace too much, and the smaller, patchy dog only looked at Ace with curiosity. Neither of them growled in return. *More displaced pets.*

The man began to get back onto his bicycle.

"One more thing before you go—are those your dogs?"

"Hell, no," he said and pedaled away.

The two dogs remained, staring at her, not certain if they should follow. She kept an eye on the guy's retreating form as she reached into her pocket and pulled out a handful of dry peanut butter cereal that she'd used to coax Ace with earlier. She tossed a handful into the street, and although the scrawny dogs shied away at first, they scampered back to sniff out the offering. She continued to toss them tidbits to eat as she watched the guy disappear around the corner. He never looked back as he escaped the strange scene he'd stumbled upon, and she hoped she wouldn't see him again. "La côte est clair," she said loud enough for the girls to hear, letting them know the coast was clear.

10

Treasures

LATER THAT AFTERNOON, SHE AND THE GIRLS WERE IN LARRY'S house, using their own warped sheets of plywood to patch up the hole left by the broken sliding glass door. Once finished, they still had the Millers' to do, and already the drill was complaining. "Mae, look in the garage and see if Larry has another one of these," Sloane said as she held up the drill's battery pack.

"Got it," Mae said as Sally followed the girl to the garage.

"What's it look like out there, Wren?" she called from the back of the house.

"Nothing new, Mom. I like this one," Wren said about the yellow Labrador whom they had discovered was named Oakley according to the metal name tag on his collar. He kept watch by Wren's side and leaned into her as she stroked his soft fur.

"Just make sure you're keeping watch." Sloane smiled to herself and shook her head when Mae returned with empty hands. "I don't see anything like that," she said.

"Great. We'll have to use nails and a hammer. Problem is that it'll be easier to bust through with nails. They'd have to work at it more with the screws."

Wren's voice beckoned from the living room. "Mom, remember that time when Dad lit a light bulb with the car battery? Or the time he hooked up the TV to the battery when we went camping? Can we use the battery in Larry's truck to charge the screwdriver's battery unit?"

She thought about the process. "Hmm, interesting idea. Your dad used an inverter to light the bulb using the car battery. It's worth a try at least. Great suggestion, Wren," Sloane said. It was amazing the things kids picked up when you thought they couldn't care less. Finn had been a geeky science teacher before he became a principal and he'd often shown the girls the wonder of science, just as she taught them French growing up. *Oh, how she missed him.*

Once, on a Saturday morning, she woke to hear Finn using her hairdryer to hover and spin a little white Ping-Pong ball as Wren's four-year-old eyes beheld the wonder and believed her father a magician. Just like the Ping-Pong ball, she also recalled the light bulb incident. She had gone to retrieve frozen lasagna out of the garage freezer one afternoon and was surprised to find him holding a bright light bulb over the car's engine. Again, her girls looked at him as if he was capable of conjuring anything with his bare hands.

They left Larry's place with their dog procession in tow, and once they returned to their own garage, Sloane quickly located the inverter. Finn had stashed it away years before under his workbench in a waterproof plastic tub, and once again, she was relieved that Brady had no interest in the garage or Finn's tools.

She left the girls to keep watch with the mudroom door open while she worked. She lifted the hood of her floodwater ruined minivan and connected the negative clamp of the inverter and then the positive. She then prayed the little LED green light would turn on when she turned the inverter around, and it did; the little bulb glowed green. "YES!"

That told her two things: one, she could charge the screwdriver's battery pack and two, all the auto batteries in the neighborhood's abandoned vehicles were a valuable commodity, even if the autos themselves were worthless. She needed to collect the batteries and hide them or keep them under guard before someone tried to relieve her of them.

The thought panicked her a bit, envisioning bicycle man making off with her battery under his arm. *One thing at a time*, she eased herself.

She plugged the cordless screwdriver's recharging unit into the inverter and affixed the dead battery inside. The red charging light flashed off and on, indicating the battery was in the process of charging.

I have smart girls. We might make it through this, yet.

"Mom," Mae called.

"Yes?"

"What are we going to feed the dogs next? They're sniffing around the kitchen."

They had four dogs now—one for each house. She'd gladly take in a few more strays for extra insurance if she could find them. "We only feed them in their own houses. We should try to make use of the spoiled food in each house first. That way, they'll gladly separate from the pack, go inside, and stay the night. So don't feed them anything out of the kitchen here. We're the bringers of food and good things. We'll go around and check the hoses again after we finish boarding up Larry's house and then check to see what's available for each dog to eat."

She left the battery to charge and returned to the living room as Ace came to greet her. She really liked this dog. She scratched him around the scruff of his neck and under his collar. "Good boy, Ace." He panted at her and she would have sworn he smiled.

"Great idea, Wren. It's working. The drill's battery is charging. We should be able to finish the work on both houses today."

Wren smiled and stood a little taller. Sloane thought about how crazy it was. *We're in the worst of situations and we're—happy? Almost as happy as we were with Finn.*

"Mom, if that works, could we run a fan, too?" Mae asked.

"Uh, no. We can't use the power for comfort, only necessities."

"I figured you'd say that," Mae complained.

"There are worse things than being hot, Mae—like being hungry. Let's keep our priorities in order."

"Mom! I hear something," Wren warned.

The dogs heard it, too. Baxter—the shorter of the new dogs—began to howl. They hadn't heard the sound in days, but it seemed like weeks. The main highway going through town rumbled, a mere vibration on the wave of the air. A minute sound they knew they were missing before, yet couldn't name now. They only knew that it was too quiet. With its presence again, it stood out sorely and obtrusively in the peace they'd already learned to savor.

"Is it traffic noise?" Mae asked with uncertainty.

"Most vehicles are so water damaged, they don't work now. It must be the military trying to get things back together," she said with hope, but inside she wasn't sure if it was a good idea or not. She was afraid of what the government might make of them—those who survived on their own and didn't need their help. She didn't want to go to a FEMA camp and she certainly didn't want her girls in one. She'd take to the forest if it came to that. Or she'd fool them in some way with the hope of remaining on Horseshoe Lane.

11

Planning

ONCE THE DOORWAYS WERE ALL BOARDED UP AND THE draining hoses rechecked, they went inside each house and retrieved all the automobile batteries. They also emptied the refrigerators, freezers, and pantries and then separated items into three categories—for humans, for the dogs, and too far gone for even the dogs.

Most of the refrigerated produce, like moisture-rich radishes and lettuce, was long spoiled. Dogs would eat even fuzzy, bendable carrots if they chopped them up and used them in homemade dog food. Sloane remembered Brian Miller explaining how dogs only really needed three basic ingredients. Their food consisted of a third each of protein, grain, and vegetable. His mother had always cooked his boyhood canines' food once a week, opting for chopped chicken, rice, and whatever vegetable young Brian refused to eat at the evening meal. They kept it in a container in the refrigerator and doled it out twice a day to the dog.

Never before was Sloane more thankful for the yammering of Brian Miller. This story came back to her as an epiphany. She could use all the leftovers and categorize them into portions, dishing them out morning and night.

In each kitchen, after separating what would go to the dogs, they made sure to combine these thirds into a large bowl before mixing them up thoroughly. The vegetarian household of the Carsons posed little problem as they still found leftover tofu to use for the protein and even what looked to be a thawing tuna casserole in the deep freezer. Ace didn't seem to care and these things easily mixed together. That evening as they put the dogs away in each home, ensuring them of their good fortune, they fed them the lavish treat and gave them each a blanket to sleep upon.

Ace went back to the Carsons'; Oakley, the lab, to Larry's house; Baxter went to the Millers'; and they kept little Sally at their own home. Sloane made sure to alternate the opened windows and added solar lanterns in a different room of each house. They also checked the bags on Brian Miller's blueberry bushes as the sun began to fade away. There was a third of a cup of water in each bag. Though it wasn't much, it was a successful experiment that she would expand on. Although the hot days of summer were scorching, she recognized she could count on finding ways to survive by utilizing a few tricks.

That evening, as they ate the last of their own salvaged leftovers, she and the girls felt the sore muscles they didn't know they had before. Tomorrow, she would venture upstairs into her attic food stores.

"Now what, Mom?" Mae asked. "We're armed. We have the canine brigade and we've boarded up the other houses. What's our next priority?"

Her girls ate at the makeshift table while she watched the

street below. She chewed a few more times than necessary, stalling. "Security is always our number one concern. We'll have different problems each day, like we did this morning. We can't become complacent. What works today may not work for tomorrow, so we have to adapt and plan for contingencies. As for the houses, we still need to finish draining the basements. They've gone down six more inches today, and that's great, but we're already having problems with mold growing on the walls. We'll have to use bleach to take care of that because it's really unhealthy for us."

She wasn't watching the girls as she spoke, but when they giggled, she turned and saw that they were watching Sally. Sally stood on her back feet, front paws together, while she waved them up and down in unison. She'd only seen this poodle behavior in videos before.

"What is she doing?" Wren asked.

"She's begging," Sloane answered. "Poodle breeds do that. They endear themselves for treats. It's a survival technique."

"Have some dignity, Sally," Mae playfully chastised.

"You two get some sleep. We have to trade watches again tonight."

As the girls turned in, Sloane stifled a long yawn. The exhaustion was hard to escape, but she had to keep going. Their lives depended on it.

Out there, through the darkened window, each house remained silent. At first, she'd worried the dogs might bark at night and attract attention instead of repelling it. Having the dogs on patrol with her during the day helped run off their energy and exhaustion enabled them to sleep at night. She left the window and patrolled the others on each side of the house. With the lanterns off inside, she had near-perfect night vision and was able to take in every moonlit reflection. Watching, waiting, and hoping the next few days were as easily dealt with she realistically feared that survival instincts would soon send out the worst of mankind. She would guard her place on Horseshoe Lane. She would stand her ground. *Even if I have to kill*, she told herself...believing herself capable would still take some convincing.

12

Doug

"DADDY, I'M HUNGRY." NICOLE WHISPERED THE FORBIDDEN words.

Doug watched down the street through the window at the side of the house. He hadn't seen Trent, but he knew he was there —watching and waiting to come and take what he had saved up over the years. With the kitchen's butcher knife lying over his lap, he remained vigilant, swaying back and forth in his chair. Nicole had ghosted into the room again. He knew she was there, behind him in the dark. He hated that sneakiness about her.

"You know the rules, Nicole. You had your meal earlier. That's all you get today. You can have some more tomorrow. We have to save it. I told you that. We don't know how long this will last. I saved you last time this happened, after your mother and the rest died, and I'll save you again. You'll be okay, trust me."

"That was yesterday, Daddy. Don't you remember? You fed me

yesterday. I haven't had anything today. Not even water. I'm so hungry. I think you forget sometimes, but it's not your fault...Dad? My stomach hurts and we have lots of food stored everywhere. Can't I have maybe a little? I won't eat much, just a small can, I promise."

"I told you, no!" he yelled shaking in anger, pounding his fist into the chair that he had faced directly in front of his lookout window. She dropped to her knees in a sob. He hated it when she cried and begged. He was keeping her alive. She should be thankful. He had to keep her alive and, even if she lost weight, she wouldn't starve to death and neither would he. "Don't be greedy, Nicole. Go to bed now." She left the way she came, silently drifting through the house like a ghost.

Trent would come and take his food stores, but he was waiting for him this time. He hadn't slept more than a wink since this all started. Except for the one time Nicole slipped away. He'd seen her walking home with that damn cat. As if they could spare anything for an animal.

"Daddy, can I keep him?" she had asked.

Why didn't she understand what he was doing was for her own survival? He needed to protect his daughter, especially from Trent Carson.

He hadn't slept for three days and even then, he dared not shut his eyes for an hour or more at a time. He only watched and waited, keenly aware of the danger Trent posed.

"Hurry up, you bastard. Come and get it. I'm waiting for you this time," Doug mumbled.

"What, Daddy?" Nicole asked a moment later from the hallway.

"Nothing, Nicole. Go to bed," he repeated. He hated her staring at him from behind his back. She was just like her mother, Carey. A daily reminder of his failures. Carey blamed him from beyond the grave, he knew it. She berated him from beyond as she did in life. He heard her mostly from the basement, near the bulkhead doorway where he'd stored her body—and those of their other children—four years ago.

Carey didn't like it down there. It was too cold in the winter and too damp in the summer months. Nothing would please her. She always complained, even in death. If only she'd stay down there to haunt him, he could live with that. But lately, she'd come up from the basement and spoke to him from the darkened living room. She'd stand behind him, whispering in his ear as his head nodded off. She told him Trent would come in if he slept. He would sneak in and rob them of all he'd accumulated. *He will take it all for himself*, she warned him. He would again feel the pangs of hunger, the dread of failing; he'd watch Nicole die before his eyes, and it would be all his fault, like before, she told him. He was an utter failure.

He had let them die. She'd begged him to do something. She begged him that night when he broke into Larry's house and tried to steal antivirals. That was the night Trent nearly blew his head off with the shotgun, and she watched it all from their bedroom window. It was humiliating for him.

She died the next day—but she didn't stay dead. No, she'd haunted him since then. He couldn't sell the house. He wouldn't leave her here by herself. Their other children sometimes cried at night. He could hear them even now in the distance. He couldn't abandon them in death as easily as he'd failed them in their lives.

13

Knock at the Door

THE NEXT MORNING, SLOANE AGAIN AWOKE TO MAE breathing out the word, "Mooooommm."

"Please... stop waking me that way," Sloane said. Then, startled when she heard Sally yipping at the door, exclaimed, "What? What is it?"

"Nicole is at the front door."

"Why didn't you wake me earlier?"

"We've been trying to. You don't wake up easily, Mom...seriously," Mae said.

"We haven't left the room, Mom. She's been knocking for a few minutes," Wren said.

"Should we go down and answer it?" Mae asked.

"She doesn't look good. We watched her walk down here. She stumbled most of the way and she held her stomach. I think something's wrong with her."

"Oh my God, he'd better not have hurt her," Sloane said then flew from the bed, holstered her weapon, and headed for the door. "Is Doug anywhere out there?"

"We haven't seen him," Wren said.

She tried to think. *What can I do for her?* It was a terrible dilemma and one she resented being caught in. Her father should take care of her, and yet, he was too far gone to see he was hurting his child, the last remnant he had left of his family.

It dawned on her that they were alike, she and Doug, but in very different ways completely. They'd both lost something precious during the pandemic and yet they reacted very differently to ensure the tragedy never happened again. She'd made mistakes along the way, but she recognized them for what they were.

He wallowed in his loss, allowed himself to be consumed by his hatred for Trent, and compensated for his own previous failings with material items.

Where she planned for catastrophes by filling her attic with survival food and supplies, he hoarded anything and everything, filling his home with objects to insulate the void his dead family left behind. She could only imagine what might be going on in Doug's demented mind but in any event, it wasn't good.

"I'll go down and answer the door. You two stay up here for now and keep watch. If you see her father, yell down. It might be a trick."

Both girls never considered this of Doug and they were frightened.

"Be careful, Mom," Mae said as she closed the door behind her.

"Always, dove," she said and left them to watch and to listen.

She approached the door, and instead of the girl standing where she could not see her, Nicole sat leaning against the wall, just beyond the opaque-veiled side window of the door. The girl's left arm lifted weakly and rapped the entrance once more.

Oh my God! What has he done to her?

She slid back the curtain and expected to see blood. Nicole hadn't noticed her peering down at her. She had her eyes closed, and Sloane thought she must be barely conscious, as she'd gone from sitting to lying on the concrete stoop.

Sloane peeked around the doorframe, half-expecting to see Doug trying to ambush her. The day was so new, only a sliver of dawn greeted them yet. She peered down again at the girl who was now resting, having given up on trying to get the attention she sought.

Sloane opened the door a crack, but Nicole didn't stir when the hinge creaked. Her skinny legs, in the same outfit as the days before, stuck out like twigs. Her knees appeared swollen, her arms too long for her frame.

"Nicole?" she spoke to her as she knelt down. "Nicole?"

She had not yet responded, and Sloane reached a hand out to touch her arm. Her large blue eyes, underlined with dark blue circles and splotches of red, fluttered open, sunken and too big for her face. She peered up at Sloane as if she didn't recognize where she was.

"Sloane. Hi," Nicole labored to say with chapped lips and without moving her body. Her dull eyes again, too difficult to keep open, shut on their own.

She's dehydrated.

"Let's get you inside, Nicole." She found herself ignoring the advice in her own head and spoke without thinking, but she couldn't leave her like this. She holstered her gun to lift the girl and briefly thought, *If it is a trick of Doug's doing, now would be the time he'd attack.* She watched for it as she lifted the girl. She was shockingly light for a twelve-year-old child. When nothing happened, Sloane kicked the door shut and locked the deadbolt while Nicole's head began to slip from her shoulder, dangling down awkwardly.

She struggled to get the girl to the couch.

"Mae. Get some water, quick."

She laid Nicole down on her once-soft moleskin sofa, now rough and scratchy from the seawater wash.

"Nicole," she called while patting the girl's sunken cheek. She'd lost consciousness altogether.

How could he do this to her? She screamed inside herself.

Mae came down the stairs in a hurry, with Sally right beside her. Wren appeared at the top of the stairs and asked, "Is she okay?"

"Why aren't you watching?" Sloane yelled at Wren and then chastised herself. "I'm sorry. Please keep looking out. Tell me if you see him."

"Sorry Mom," Wren said, distraught, and disappeared quickly into the bedroom once again.

Sloane knew her daughter was only worried for young Nicole, but now wasn't the time. Doug might come out of his demented lair and attack them at any moment. She needed to be forewarned. She'd kill him if he tried to break in. She'd kill him if he tried to take Nicole from them. She'd made the promise. She intended to keep it.

14

Nicole

NICOLE HAD WAITED UNTIL THE EARLY MORNING HOURS TO leave. She hadn't slept at all. Her stomach ached and her bedroom spun whenever she tried to walk. Even as she snuck down the blue-lit hallway, it seemed to tilt and she walked in the corner crevice as the ceiling appeared to suddenly swoop to the side.

Later, she was woken on the dirty flooring by the snores of her father in the living room chair. He hadn't left his spot there for days. He reeked—she suspected he'd wet himself or worse. He talked to himself more and more over the past year, but the last several days were the worst she'd seen him. Sometimes he was fine for days at a time; then she'd come home from school and find him crying to himself in the basement. She left him alone; if she didn't, he'd hit her sometimes. She didn't think he remembered the episodes but she did.

The hoarding started when she was a small girl. She hadn't thought it strange at the time, but it became worse as the years went on. Some of the kids made fun of her for it and she didn't know what to say to them. No one came over to play with her anymore. She'd heard the whispers of parents refusing to let their children reciprocate a play date. She could come over to their house anytime, but no one would come to her home to play. She couldn't blame them.

She remembered what starving was like during the pandemic, but this was worse. He wouldn't even let her have the stored water and when he'd caught her with her head under the sink faucet, trying out of desperation to drink only a mouthful, he'd slapped her. The shock of it stung her. She loved him, he was her dad, yet he lived in a different world than her in their own home. He didn't remember much from one day to the next, and she knew if she were to survive, she'd have to leave him here alone. Leave him to the world he created in his own mind. Once she was well enough, she'd come back for him and maybe she'd be able to reach him. For now, though, she needed to get help for herself. She had to or they'd both die.

So she lifted herself from her bedroom floor and went through the open sliding glass door he hadn't bothered to fix. She stumbled through the dawn and wound her way around strewn debris, her vision only a pinpoint within her sticky eyes. She stumbled and fell when the world threatened to defy her as before. The air smelled better outside though, and the chilly morning wind put goose bumps on her bare arms.

Finally, she made it to Sloane's driveway, though she barely remembered the trip. Sloane had said the Carsons were home, but she still didn't see anyone so she had continued on to Sloane's and knocked on the wooden door. *Maybe no one is home. It's so quiet.*

Then, as before, the horizon twisted. Little white sparks of light flashed in her eyes and then darkness began to close in on her. She slid down the wall, waiting. *Maybe they'll come.*

15

A Visitor

THEY'D PUT HER IN MAE'S ROOM DOWN AT THE END OF THE long hallway and closed the door for now. She mumbled things here and there but had yet to regain full consciousness.

"Remember, if we see him, we don't know where she is," Sloane insisted. "We'll just tell him we haven't seen her at all. We must go about our day as if everything is normal so he doesn't suspect we're involved."

"Okay, but how long can we keep that up? We can't hide her forever," Mae said.

"We'll do it for as long as it takes. She can't go back there. Wren, you keep watch and if you hear anything, yell. We'll do our rounds, check to see if the basements are draining, and come back as soon as possible."

"Okay," Wren said.

Sloane had mixed small electrolyte packages from her food stores with water and they'd poured trickles of it into the girl's mouth at short intervals. She swallowed and managed to keep it down so Sloane decided to do it again in an hour's time and hoped the girl regained consciousness soon. For now, they made their way across the street and let Ace outside. He did his business while she and Mae checked the hoses. Mae kept watch while Sloane had her back turned.

So far, none of the other remaining neighbors had shown themselves, and she suspected most of them had fled around the same time the Carsons did. Still, she couldn't be certain, and that was why they needed to maintain vigilance. Of all the people she wouldn't want to end up on the block alone with, it was Doug Sperry. Unfortunately, though, that appeared to be exactly what had happened.

"Okay Mae, I think the basements are over half empty. By this time next week, we'll begin scrubbing the walls and straightening things up."

"Great Mom. I can't wait to smell like bleach," Mae said. She could always count on Mae to come up with something dour.

"It gives us purpose, Mae, don't you see?"

"No... but whatever you say," Mae said.

"That's my girl."

Once they'd finished and the canine brigade was assembled, Mae tried to trick them with a ball. She pretended to toss it as the four animals sat on their haunches, watching her. She mock-threw the ball but hid it behind her back. Oakley, Sally, and Ace all jetted toward the phantom ball while Baxter, the unsuspecting mutt with the spotted coat, trotted behind her after having spotted the secret Mae hid behind her back.

Sloane chuckled, again finding 'joy in the journey'.

"You're the smartest dog," Mae said.

"Okay, come inside so I can check on her." Sloane didn't want to say Nicole's name out loud for fear that Doug could be watching them and hear her.

She locked the door, and as the dogs milled around on the main floor, Sloane ran up the steps. "How is it, Wren?"

"Fine, Mom. I haven't seen anything."

"Have you heard Nicole at all?"

"Nope. I think she's still sleeping. We're not going to let her go back to him, are we? She's in really bad shape."

She didn't know what to say. That depended on Nicole, but for now the answer was *no*.

"We'll get her well and make that decision later."

She left Wren on watch and then approached Mae's room. She opened the door and found the girl blinking open her eyes.

"Nicole. Hi sweetheart. How are you feeling?"

She looked confused, like she didn't know where she was, which of course, she didn't. "Where am I?"

"Do you remember coming down here this morning?"

She took her time to answer. "I think so."

"Do you know where your father is?"

"He's asleep in his chair."

"When's the last time you've eaten anything?"

"It's been a while. He's...confused. He forgets that I haven't eaten."

She helped the girl sit up and made her drink more of the electrolyte water.

"After you finish this, I'll give you a little oatmeal if you feel like you can keep it down."

"Thank you, Sloane," Nicole said and would have cried had she the tears to spare.

"Nicole, it's okay. Don't get upset. We need to get you well." She knelt down after hugging the girl and sat at her level. She needed to have an agreement with the girl if she was going to be able to help her long term.

"Listen. Your father's having some problems. He may come here looking for you. If he does, I want you to hide if you hear his voice. Can you do that for me?"

"He's...he's not well. He doesn't mean to hurt me..." she tried to explain.

"I know, Nicole. You don't need to make excuses. I understand, trust me I do, but you must survive and in order to do that, you need to save yourself from him. So if he shows up here looking for you, you need to keep quiet and hide. I'll come up with an excuse. Once you're better, we'll talk about what to do next, okay?"

She hoped the girl would go for it, but the emotional strain was too much and the girl's eyes became heavier. She slid down into the veil of sleep again and Sloane covered her back up. In another hour, she'd get her to drink more liquid and try a little oatmeal, a little at a time.

Not one second after she shut the bedroom door, she heard Wren's alarmed voice. "Mooom!"

She doubled her steps and ran to her room.

"What?"

"He's coming," Wren warned.

Sloane sidled up to the window. Doug walked side to side at a quick pace. In his right hand, a butcher knife swung back and forth. He swiped at his own leg as he went.

"Mae, get up here. Now." She hefted the AR-10 and chambered a round before handing it to Mae and positioning her to aim at the door. Wren already held the shotgun. "No matter what you hear, do not leave this room. If he enters, shoot him. Empty every bullet you have into him. Don't stop at one. I love you both." She quickly left and locked the door behind her before they could cry.

She reached the front door right as he began pounding on it.

"Sloane...Sloane!" he yelled.

She had her Glock and the other pistol out and ready.

"What, Doug?"

"Open the door. I need to talk to you," Doug said.

He sounded scared and Sloane almost felt sympathy for the man, but not enough to endanger herself or her children.

"I'm afraid I can't do that, Doug," she said.

"Sloane...Sloane...listen to me," he said and then Ace ran up to the window, having recognized the danger in the man's voice. He growled at Doug through the glass and followed with vicious barks.

"You're not safe with Trent here. He's trying to take everything I have. Once he takes all of my stuff, he'll come after you." He paused as though trying to remember something. "Oh, and Nicole's gone. I can't find her. I think he took her, too. You haven't seen her, have you?"

She bit her lip. He was truly insane. Even though Nicole was missing, his stuff still came before his child.

"No Doug. I haven't seen her. I talked with Trent earlier today. He's been busy cleaning his basement. He's not concerned with you, Doug. Try to calm down. I'm sure Nicole will wander back home later tonight or tomorrow. Don't worry about her. If she shows up, I'll send her home. Okay?"

"I'm warning you, Sloane. He'll kill you for everything you have. You better listen to me. I'm going to get him before he gets me. This time I'll get him..." he said as his voice trailed away to a mumble.

Ace barked again and growled at his retreating form.

She peeked around the doorframe and looked through the window to where he had stood. Red droplets of blood stained her concrete stoop. Perfect rounds of crimson red marked a splattered trail both to and from her door. She could not let Nicole go back with him. She'd have to continue the deception.

16

Priorities

THE DAY TURNED TO NIGHT, AND SHE DIDN'T WANT TO LEAVE the girls. After Nicole woke again, she fed her a half cup of oatmeal watered down with reconstituted milk. She'd hoped this would be gentle enough for her to keep down. Nicole fell asleep again, having never been alerted to her father's presence earlier. Sloane thought it was best this way. Once the girl was better, they'd figure out what to do with her, but living with Doug in his current state was out of the question.

Wren said she had watched as Doug shut himself back inside his house, gnarly knife and all, and hadn't left the residence again. They kept up the vigil, but as the evening came, Sloane decided to take the dogs back to their designated houses.

She went alone this time since the girls were scared after what they'd witnessed earlier in the day. She'd left both of her daughters locked in her room, as before, with the same orders. *If Doug shows up here, shoot him dead.* She set up the neighbors' yards in a different arrangement than the night before and waved to Wren whenever she could to ease her fears. She had to keep up the illusion that Trent was home or Doug would be at her door again in the morning.

She needed to recheck the hoses, feed the dogs, and lock up for the night. She'd begun varying her routine so that no one watching could surprise her. This time, she began with the Millers, who now had a solar lantern on in their dining room, and then the Bakers, who had closed their downstairs windows and opened the upstairs ones. Finally, as she and Ace walked into the Carsons' house, it was pitch black. She and Ace were making their way to the kitchen when the tiny hairs along her neck stood up. She began to turn on her little flashlight when, all of a sudden, Ace began to growl, low and ominous. Fear shot through her in an instant.

Someone was in there, in the dark. She turned on the flashlight and saw the blood drops along the carpeted entry. *Doug!* She turned to leave when she heard him speak.

"Trent! I'm going to get you before you get me!"

She turned around and Doug was on top of her. She saw a glint of a knife above her, followed by a sudden impact and a sharp pain. She felt him tug at the handle that now was a part of her somehow. Ace lunged at him. A mauling sound made Doug pierce the night air with a high-pitched scream.

She staggered backwards and ran for the doorway. When she stumbled out into the night, the screaming and growling followed her. She drew her gun, but not before she looked down and saw the knife embedded to the hilt into her shoulder, the handle sticking out before her. The pain hit her and she fell to her knees.

Ace emitted a painful shriek from within the house. A sound erupted from the opposite side of the street and when she looked up at her own bedroom window, she saw her girls were screaming in horror and pointing behind her. She turned again and saw Doug running toward her with a murderous, deranged look on his face. He thought she was Trent. She raised the Glock and fired at him. He never slowed down. He kept coming for her. She fired again and again, and still he was coming at her. She felt the dark closing in. She was fainting and he was nearly on top of her. She fired once more and then her head fell backwards and slammed into the pavement of Horseshoe Lane.

Her eyes flickered toward the girls in the window. Their mouths agape, she could no longer hear their screams. Her own heartbeat was somehow too loud and crowded out their cries. Above her, the stars twinkled, the moon was full and bright, and then it all died out into the night.

17

Wren in Chaos

"Mom! Mom!" Wren yelled as she stood on the second floor. Her damp hands held the shaking rifle, as her sister screamed over and over and, Nicole kept roaring, "No!"

That was when the sisters' mother ran from the darkened house with the hilt of a knife sticking out of the space just below her left clavicle with Nicole's father chasing her. Then the shots were fired, as their mother lay in the middle of the street on her back, with momentary flashes that lite the night in contrast to the dark in rapid bursts.

Without the moonlight, the three girls would not have known the final outcome, but they saw everything...even the last moment Sloan looked up at them in the window to the moment when Doug's body landed face down across her legs. Like a drunken boat docking at a busy marina on a Saturday night, Sloan's body jolted to the side, then righted once again with the impact.

That was it. Both bodies laid motionless. Still. Wren put the rifle down, leaned it against the wall, thinking, *How can you leave us like this? You promised.*

"Mom! Is she dead?" Mae turned to Wren and asked. Tears streaming down her face, her hands plastered to the window.

Nicole had turned away, leaned against the wall, buckled into herself and slid down the wall wracked with sobs when Wren looked.

She didn't blame Nicole, she couldn't look at them laying there in the street any longer, either.

"Where are you going?" Mae screamed. "Mom said to stay *here*."

Before Wren realized her plan, she unlocked the door to the bedroom and rushed downstairs with Mae on her heels.

"You can't go out there!" Mae yelled.

"We have to get Mom away from him. Now help me or be quiet!" she said through clenched teeth.

Nicole suddenly appeared next to Mae saying, "We can help," as she rubbed the slick moisture away from her eyes with the palms of her hands.

I can't let her see her father that way, Wren thought. *It's not right.*

"Nicole, no. You should stay here. Mae and I...we'll bring Mom in."

As Nicole began to shake her head in protest, Wren said, "We need you to look out for anyone. We'll be quick. Yell if you see anyone coming, okay?"

The young girl took in a long shuttering breath. The breath told Wren, the tears were held there...just on the verge.

"I knew something like this was going to happen." Wren's harsh whisper caught her sister by surprise.

"How did *you* know?" Mae asked still crying.

"Just get behind me. Only move when I say so," Wren said. She put her warm hand on the door handle, and looked out the side window with the two bodies lying there in the street. A silver-winged moth floated down like a feather and landed on corpses as if that were allowed now that her mother was motionless out there. Wren opened the door, then felt Mae's clammy hands hang onto her arm. "Stop that! Come on," she said, shaking from her sister's grasp.

Looking up and down the street as she neared the stoop, she saw no movement. Nothing. No one came running to help them or harm them. *If moths could land on corpses in the middle of the street, no one is coming, friend or foe*, she reasoned.

Then, when she decided to stop being afraid, Wren marched with heed, straight out to her mother.

"Wait, is it safe?" Mae said scrambling after her sister. "Mom said to stay inside!"

Wren never answered. Her feet stopped at her mother's head while her arms hung like stiff rods swinging at her sides.

Standing over her mother's form from the top down, it occurred to Wren that never in her life had she seen her mother this way: small, delicate, fragile. Dead? That was the question Mae asked her earlier. The hilt swayed just so slightly in the wind. Wren's knees buckled suddenly, to get a closer look. "Mom?"

"Is she dead?" Mae asked, her voice wretched, from five broad steps behind her.

Wren forgot her sister. Forgot she was even there.

"No. Help me."

"Is he...dead?" Mae asked still from the same distance behind her.

"Yes. Too much blood."

Pebbles skidded under the soles Mae's sneakers as Wren's eyes tracked the slow oscillations of the hilt, back and forth. It wasn't the wind.

"Be careful of the knife," Wren said to her sister as they each lifted their mother by the shoulders and freed her legs of the dead weight of Doug.

She felt her mother would weigh as much as a mountain. She thought the task of dragging her inside the house would take all night. In no time, they pulled her surprisingly light body, back across the street, out of the moonlight and into the darkened house.

It was Nicole who held the door open to the moonlight as they crossed the threshold and sealed it slowly shut as she peeked at her dead father's form until the last sliver blinked out.

18

A Mantra

"What do we do now?" Mae asked as the three of them stared down at Sloan's body on the living room floor.

"I don't know. I'm not a doctor," Wren yelled.

"We can't call a doctor," Nicole whispered. "I'm sorry. I'm sorry he did this to your mom."

"Stop crying. Both of you," Wren said, annoyed, as the younger girls embraced. "It's not your fault, Nicole. It's no one's fault. *She* shouldn't have gone over there."

"It's not Mom's fault!" Mae yelled.

"Shut up!" Wren yelled and knelt down near her mother's head with her eyes affixed to the knife handle still swaying in the wind.

"Get some clean towels...and, a bottle of water," Wren said and both girls ran off, returning quickly with the items.

Wren took one of the clean white hand towels their mother kept only for guests and sat the others nearby. "She's not going to like that we used her best towels," she said as she reached for the handle when Mae suddenly asked, "Wait! What are you gonna do?"

Retracting her hand suddenly, Wren said, "I'm going to pull out the knife, Mae. What do you think I'm going to do? We can't leave it in there like that."

"Shouldn't we wait for someone?" Mae asked.

"We can't *wait* for someone. There is no *someone*. It's just us, Mae. Here, hold this towel. As soon as I pull out the knife, you put the towel on the wound and push down. That's what they told us in health class."

"Okay," Mae said kneeling down next to Wren's side and holding the folded towel shaking in her hands.

Wren hadn't touched the knife handle yet. She still gazed at its sway. That movement meant her mother breathed but what would happen when she pulled the blade free? Did the sharp point pierce a lung? The blood, she expected, but what about after that? What if she stopped breathing then? Wren closed her eyes and shook her head.

Don't get ahead of yourself. Don't over think. One step at a time. That's what Wren's father used to say to her at the kitchen table as he guided her through tough math problems. It became a mantra for Wren before tests. Now, the mantra played on a loop within her mind. *Don't get ahead of yourself. Don't over think. One step at a time.*

Her hand reached for the hilt. That's when she literally felt her mother's life within her hand. She grasped the handle harder.

"Wait, Wren, maybe..."

And Wren pulled the knife free with one swift yank.

Blood pooled up and began soaking the circumference of the wound. "Now, Mae. The towel."

"Oh," Mae said and reached the towel forward, "I can't."

Wren grabbed the cloth from her sister and pushed the layers into her mother's shoulder. Kneeling up, she pressed down.

Then nothing. No one said a word, as if it was any other dull day in the living room playing a game or reading a book. But Wren watched her mother's chest as she held her down. She waited for the rise and ebb of her mother's breathing. She felt for it, too.

"It's getting on the carpet," Nicole said pointing a finger down at the once beige rug, turned a dark grey after the flooding, and now the damaged fibers were evolving into a shade of maroon.

"Oh, help me," Wren said, and the three of them rolled Sloane onto her side, placing a pad of towels underneath her shoulder. Turning her back again, Wren pushed down on the wound.

After a time, Wren lifted her palm and saw the bloom of bright red blood growing beneath. "Hand me another towel."

"Is it stopping? What do we do if it doesn't stop?"

"We'll keep adding towels until it does, Mae."

"Won't that soak up *all* her blood? I don't think we have enough towels," Mae said suddenly startled.

"Mae, it's okay. She's breathing, see?" she said pointing to her mother's chest. "And her pulse is beating. She's going to be all right."

"Why is she still sleeping then?" Nicole asked.

Wren hadn't asked herself that question, yet. Looking down at her mother, the scene replayed in her mind.

Her mother came out of the house with the knife hilt already stuck inside her. She ran down into the street. She staggered and then fell as she shot Nicole's father a few times. That's when Wren remembered seeing her mother's head hit the pavement. Watched the scene replay in her mind, the sickening thud as the back her mother's skull slammed down on the road. That was called a concussion, a brain injury. That was bad.

With her clean hand, Wren slipped it under the back of her mother's head, massaged her scalp, and felt there. She pulled it away and came back clean.

"We have to wait and see. We don't know what's going to happen yet."

19

Two Weeks Later

"Moooom," Mae woke her.

"I swear to God, you've got to stop that, Mae! Is there something wrong?"

"No, I was only joking," Mae giggled.

"That is not funny. Is everyone up?"

"Yeah, Nicole's on watch and Wren's fixing breakfast," Mae said as she helped her mother sit up, though she didn't need to now. She did it more out of kindness than necessity.

Her left shoulder was still bandaged. The going was slow in the first few days, but now the wound was healing quickly. She had no idea how much damage there was internally, only that it hurt like hell from time to time.

"Anything to report, Wren?"

"Not really. We heard a convoy go by again about an hour ago. It's happening more and more each day. What do you think that means?" her daughter asked.

"I don't know. It's either a very good thing or a very bad thing. We have plans to stay here, but if it comes to anyone trying to make us leave, we still have a contingency plan to leave. Let's keep listening for now."

"All right, Mom," Wren said.

She hadn't been conscious when the girls slipped out of their hiding places and defied their mother's orders that night. Wren pulled the knife from her mother's unconscious body after they brought her inside. They poured peroxide over the stab wound and cleaned it up, but they didn't attempt to sew up the four-inch long gash. Instead, they closed the wound the best they could with lengths of medical tape from their first-aid kit and kept it as clean as possible. Wren also fished out the stored antibiotics Sloane had stashed in the attic along with the food.

She'd awoken to Nicole weeping at her side the next morning, expelling tears she didn't have. She was afraid the girl was going to be angry with her over her father's death—surprisingly, she wasn't.

Although she loved her father, Nicole had agreed that Doug had lost his mind four years ago. She took comfort in knowing he was now with the rest of her deceased family, at peace finally. She was free of him and his torment.

Sloane officially invited Nicole to live with them after that, and she had accepted. Not that there was anywhere for her to go, but Sloane wanted it to be her choice.

Over the last two weeks, they'd come up with a better system to maintain their Horseshoe Lane deception. Sloane involved the kids in the planning. The game kept their minds working and was something for them to dream about.

Each day, someone was responsible for a different yard-scape using items from each of the homes. Trent Carson was often responsible for leaving lawn chairs and beer bottles strewn in different scenic positions of his front yard. They were talking about an intervention. The warning sign he'd created to warn people off was found in his garage and predominantly displayed in all its juvenile arts and crafts glory.

Larry was starting on front porch repairs. Several two-by-fours lingered alongside cans of paint.

The Millers were now experimenting with fall crop gardening. Several areas of their front lawn were pulled up and being readied for planting. All of the homes now sported little clear baggies tied to branches of nontoxic leaves. They were collected by different people wearing different hats each evening.

As Sloane began the day, she watched while Nicole threw the ball down the road. Six of their canine friends leapt after it in unison. She looked down at Sally by her feet. "You don't fetch balls, do you?" If she could answer, Sloane knew the little dog would say, "No, that is below my station in life."

To her left, Ace sat contentedly; he'd kept her company after the injury and never left her side. He'd limped back to the main house after the girls carried her inside. Doug had kicked him terribly as he tried to get away from his attacker. If it hadn't been for Ace, there was no way Doug would have let her go and, instead, would have sunk the knife into her again. Those thoughts ran through her mind over and over. What would have become of her girls then?

"You're a good boy, Ace. The best boy ever," she said and scratched him behind the neck. He still limped but, like her, he was getting a little better each day.

The hardest part was dealing with Doug's body. He'd lain in the road for two days and she couldn't stand to have Nicole at the window, seeing her own father there as the birds pecked at his flesh. She disposed of him with only Ace as her accomplice. After the younger girls had gone to sleep, she left Wren on watch while she took Ace with her and tipped Doug over onto a wagon they found at the Millers'. It took her a long time, but she had half the night to do it. She tugged and bartered with whoever might be listening from above to give her strength and fortitude.

She finally made it to what she thought of now as the cemetery in the woods. She dragged him till her shoulder bled though her shirt again, to the same spot Brady's decomposing corpse still lay. She thought she should say a few words, but nothing came to her. She was empty of words for the dead so she and Ace stood there, listening to the quiet. After a while, they turned and started for home. Then, as before, she heard rustling in the bushes and out came a few more pets to lead home. Ace made sure they were worthy, and they followed them back to Horseshoe Lane. Their pack had grown.

She kept watch this morning as the girls worked on the Bakers' house. The Carsons' home had already been remediated of mold. They'd sprayed and scrubbed the walls with a combination of sink water and bleach. The home had been swept out, the furniture replaced, and other than the dining room table screwed to the Carson's wall, everything looked more or less normal after a wall of water ran through it.

She'd come to the conclusion, after she surpassed the fear, that everything was going to be okay. This life on her own, without Finn, was hard but she could do it. She'd proven that.

Now that things were getting back to normal, they waited. The others would return someday, and when they did, their homes would be waiting for them. She had saved them, but more importantly, they had saved her.

And then it happened one night...

20

Stock-Still Terror

Three months later, Sloane whispered, "Don't...make...a...sound."

Sloane's girls couldn't see their mother in the darkened bedroom, but they knew to heed her every whispered word metered out with care.

A funny smell hung in the air, one that caused them to breathe in momentarily, halting their breath in an effort to refuse something. That was what first stirred Sloane from a light, guarded sleep. Then, the sounds of footsteps on the creaky staircase wrought by a saltwater invasion and slowly dried over the months, loosening the screws so that anyone with a feathers weight sounded an orchestrated alarm. This noise brought her around completely, knowing it was more than the wind. When she sat up, through bleary eyes, she saw their bedroom door was locked as always and yet, a lightbeam shone like a laser through the cracks from the other side. There shouldn't be anyone there, yet there was, and that was an ominous sign since her canine friends had not barked even once or growled an alert.

With only the light of the moon shining through the window, Sloane reached over Nicole's stiff form, who was frozen stock-still in terror, and grabbed her Glock off the nightstand. The child's eyes were widened with fear and her breathing sped with a rapid pace. Sloane knew she had to do something in the next half second or they might all die.

Barefooted, she moved quickly to the bathroom door and motioned with her arm for the girls to follow and move as silently as possible. They'd planned this before, though this was the first time they had to actually carry out an escape from their house on Horseshoe Lane.

Her oldest daughter, Wren, ushered the two younger girls into the bathroom and Sloane barred the door behind them.

They knew not to utter a word or make the slightest sound, though Nicole held her nose to bar the odd smell that seemed stronger by the minute. She'd trained them and they'd practiced night and day for any contingency thought up. She'd made it a game amongst them to stave off boredom and to teach them survival. Sloane prayed her girls would make the short distance to safety. Their lives depended on them performing exactly as she'd taught them.

By the time the bedroom door burst open with force and yelling commenced, Sloane's bare feet were lifted high up into the false air vent which she'd previously set into place. Remembering Trent Carson's recommendation that there should always be at least two ways to escape from each room, she silently thanked him that she'd heeded this advice. Sloane had recovered the air vent before the intruders burst through the blocked doorway to the bathroom in their search for the inhabitants.

With scurrying noises only noticeable ahead of her, Sloane prayed, *Please let them make it.*

She followed them partway and when the cold, moist air hit

her face, she took a deep breath to release the odd gas odor as she made her way through the escape route in the crawlspace of the attic and soon she too was at the opening. The girls were gone though. She didn't hear a word, not one sound from them. No one screamed. The only noise she detected was within her own home as she assumed the man, or more likely men, scavenged through her supplies. *Where the heck are my dogs?*

As the freezing air stung her, Sloane peered across the side lawn fifteen feet away to the Lincolns' abandoned home which now housed their secret basement hideout. As she checked both ways through the moonlit dark for intruders, Mae's bright face reflected the moonlight in the darkness as she peeked out of the hidden entrance and Sloane was both relieved and angry as hell at the same time. *They knew better than to show themselves. That was against the rules and could get them all killed.*

Even though they were scared, she had to make them follow the plan. It meant life or death for them all. Sloane knew she needed to take care of this menace now before it was too late. Though she prepared for every single scenario she could think of, in real time, this was different. In the attic escape route, she'd hidden a bag filled with flares, matches, ammo and a pair of night vision goggles, thanks to her neighbors, the Carsons, Bakers and the Millers, who turned out to have left a plethora of survival equipment at her disposal. The only things she wished she had at the moment were shoes and perhaps a bulletproof vest and most immediately, a gas mask would be nice.

Sloane swallowed what fear began to rise from her gut and put on the night vision goggles. She heard pounding behind her and feared they were searching for their escape route. It wouldn't be long before they found her, and she was going to be ready for them when they did.

She quickly sealed up the exit the girls had taken and with her equipment, she scurried back down the path she'd come and passed the entrance to her bathroom, listening intently as she went. There were at least two of them by the sounds of it.

"The bed's still warm. They're here somewhere," she heard a muffled voice yell.

"Where the hell did they go then?"

"Hell if I know."

Sloane made out two separate male voices, muffled by masks, she guessed. They sounded like young men, not over thirty. Then one made a radio call to someone else, possibly on lookout outside and Sloane nearly panicked.

"Hey Mick, you see anything out there? They're not in here, over."

"What do you mean they're not there? We saw them in the north bedroom a few hours ago. You check the basement?"

"We cleared the whole house, man. I'm tellin' you they're gone. Did you see anything out there?"

"No, I'm watchin' the whole front of the house. Franz, any sign back there?"

So there's four of them.

"Nothing out here," Franz replied.

The next conversation really scared the hell out of her.

"All right man, it's your rear that's going to get canned when we go back to base empty-handed and report that we lost a mother and her three daughters."

"We're not empty-handed. Look, we found their rations. We'll take 'em. They can't hold out forever. They'll come walking into the FEMA camp on their own before long. It's getting colder every night. Come on. Let's go."

Then suddenly, Sloan knew what caused this.

That fat jerk! I should have killed him when I had the chance!

21

Diversion

FOR WEEKS THROUGH THE COOLING AUTUMN THE RUMBLING OF tires along the highway came as a looming threat. Sloane worried she wouldn't have everything in place by the time they discovered her and the girls within their little deception on Horseshoe Lane.

By now, out of the thirty-three homes in the neighborhood, they'd scavenged through each one and secured the doorways to keep out prowlers. They took just what they needed and ensured that they were in fact alone in the neighborhood. At first, she thought she might discover a holdout somewhere and actually hoped old Mrs. Howard might still be inside her house, but when Sloane checked over the home, she found it abandoned.

That's when reality began to hit home. She and the girls were alone and on their own...truly. It was a somber realization as the sky began to gray and snow was on the horizon. She was the only adult in charge and responsible for their sole survival, and winter seemed more a threat to her than the rumbling sounds of military trucks nearing each day.

The only news she was able to obtain from the outside world was from the occasional would-be looters who happened through her little place in this new apocalyptic world, and they were lacking more and more in ingenuity as time moved on. Their visits were lessening by the week. At first, there were several a week and then two to three. Now she found the alarms only sounded once every two to three weeks. They were typically very thin examples of their prior selves before all this started, often alone or with two or three members. They traveled on foot, skittish, dirty and malnourished. She almost felt sorry for them as she fired a few warning shots their way while they fled with her dogs chasing them out of what Sloane considered her territory. If niceties were exchanged in conversation, she asked them for the outside news in exchange for a ration. Their eyes would widen in surprise at her lack of information. The answer was always that the military was rounding up what few citizen holdouts were left and forcing them into FEMA camps. They were often surprised that she was still there, so close but apparently unaware of their presence.

There was also another threat out there, apparently; citizens that had formed a corrupt militia were also out in force and they were almost worse than the dreaded Homeland Security soldiers or whoever they claimed to be. Sloane would then thank them for their information and hasten them on their way in hopes they would go peacefully. If not, she had other methods at her disposal.

It was times like these she'd hoped that her neighbors might return for real, but now the odds were that they'd found a place to stay and though she wished she and the girls were with them for safety, she was happy for them—scared at times to be on her own but happy for them, all the same.

Then it happened while Wren was on watch late one evening. A military truck actually stopped in front of the fallen tree-barricaded neighborhood entrance. Sloane watched them through binoculars from her bedroom window as men stepped out of the Humvee and moved aside the roadblock. Sloane sent the girls into hiding as she stalked their moves. They went from house to house when she decided to pull her typical introduction ruse. She quickly left her own home to confuse the intruders into thinking she occupied another of the houses. She knelt down in the Millers' front yard garden and worked clearing away spent vegetable garden vines so desiccated mold spores blew away as she lifted them. With her rifle hidden in the debris nearby and her unloaded pistol harnessed on the outside of her right thigh, she diligently worked, ignoring their approach. She worked in the open, pulling up what remained of the tomato plants after she'd picked even the small green tomatoes to preserve for future use, and piled them to the side of the yard. When the men saw her, they approached cautiously.

"Ma'am? Put down your weapon, please."

Their guns were drawn on her as she stood and turned in their direction, her arms full of dried vines.

"Can I put these down first?"

"Just stand where you are," the loudest of them ordered.

He was a big man sporting a large belly, which was a rare sign of prosperity in these times. He motioned one of his camo-clad guys toward Sloane.

She made no sudden moves while the soldier approached her.

"Please don't move, ma'am. He's just going to secure your weapon. I'm Lieutenant Hyde."

Sloane complied with his orders, keeping her eyes on the guy in charge until she figured out what exactly he wanted.

"Is there anyone else here with you?"

"Yes, but they're not here right now."

The soldier pulled the weapon from her thigh holster and locked the Glock's slide to the rear, verifying that the chamber was empty, while she still held the Lieutenant's line of sight.

The soldier released the magazine, showing the lieutenant that it wasn't loaded, as Sloane let her armload of debris roll out of her arms and onto the ground in front of her.

The big guy huffed a little and said, "Let me get this straight. Your people left you here, alone, to clean up the garden, while they went out to scavenge."

She smiled. "It's not like that. They went in search of canning supplies while I cleaned up. We haven't had any problems here in quite a while. We mind our own business, we work hard. As you can see, we provide for our own needs."

He paced toward her as he regarded her words and seemed amused with himself. With a condescending smirk, the Lieutenant retrieved her pistol from the soldier and looked at her as if she were clueless and helpless as well. He handed the weapon back to her and then retrieved a folded piece of paper from his shirt pocket.

"Lady, you and your people are ordered to submit yourself to the FEMA camp within three days. Winter's coming and you don't want to be out here without heat and running water when that happens. We take care of everyone. You won't have to suffer through this alone. We'll relocate you to a better area when we get things under control. The government is working hard to reestablish electricity and communications. We have hospitals up and running. It's just a matter of time before everything is back to normal, a few more weeks at the most. Besides, there's still nasty characters running around out here and I'd hate to see what they'd do to *you* if they found you out here...all alone."

Sloane tried not to show her disdain for the man in front of her. The way he referred to her made her skin crawl. If anything, she was amused by his scare tactics, though she suspected humiliating a man with an ego as inflated as his would make him a raving lunatic. Instead, she did her best to feign concern and genially asked, "But if everything is going to be recovered soon, why can't we stay here until then? Just send someone to check on us every now and then, if that works."

His smile suddenly dropped. "That's not the way it works, Miss. How many are in your group?"

She stopped and thought to herself. "There's only nine adults here, and we're doing just fine by ourselves."

"Well ma'am I hope you can understand the need for your safety." He swept his arm around. "It doesn't need to be this hard to survive. We have all your needs taken care of at the camp. And we can't risk sending soldiers out here just to check on the *nine* of you.

"I'm afraid you have no choice in the matter. This is an order. Be willing to leave in three days. Pack all of your resources to take along and I'll send two trucks to help you pack."

She watched as his gaze lingered over a few of the dogs roaming freely around. She knew her best dog, Ace, was watching them closely. He wouldn't attack unless she gave the command. The Sergeant began looking a little wary of her trustworthy canines.

"I'm afraid the strays will have to be put down. We have enough abandoned dogs there. They're nothing more than a menace anyway, spreading disease and stealing resources."

Sloane didn't trust anyone that her dogs growled at. They had great taste in the human species. She scanned the paper order and nodded. "Three days?"

"Yes, is that a problem?"

She smiled again, a compliant smile this time, without a hint of deception; she'd practiced this one. "Of course. It will be a relief to us, actually. Thank you. We were becoming a little concerned about the winter weather."

She didn't like the man as soon as she'd laid eyes on him, but what he did next really cinched her lame opinion of him. He patted her on the shoulder like a good little girl.

"No worries, ma'am. I commend you on lasting as long as you have. We'll see you in three days."

Then he turned and left. She actually summoned the strength and waved at them as they departed, and then looked down at the rifle that was in plain view at her feet, before she'd dumped the spent tomato vines on top of it. She shook her head. *Don't do it.* The thought of just shooting all three of them with their guard down briefly flashed through her mind, but the moment passed. *Three days...this changes everything.*

22

An Attack

Now, squatting in the cold attic of what used to be her home as two soldiers cleaned out all of their food stores that they found while Sloane stayed patiently where she was, her warm breath freezing out before her in little clouds, she thought, *I've been so gullible. He meant to hit us earlier all along. I should have guessed. That was most likely staged. I can't believe I didn't see this coming. I thought we at least had two days to get ready. I'm such an idiot. I can't let them take us.*

And then soon, military truck tires squealed as they gained traction on the icy road. They were gone and the muscles in Sloane's thighs ached in pain and her feet were so cold they were numb. Yet, she waited and listened for a time longer to the silence and continued to mutely damn herself for overlooking the dangers before. In her crouched position, she finally turned her head toward the light and knelt farther down to her knees, sliding along her shins toward the opening. She peered outside, not trusting that they didn't leave a watcher to catch them as they came out of hiding.

Looping the canvas backpack of supplies over her shoulder, Sloane slid first one foot and then the other through the opening and stayed on alert while she rotated her ankles around until she felt the blood moving through them once again.

Confident that the girls were safe where they were for now, Sloane opted to climb down and check out what might have happened to her K-9 crew. She was afraid of what she might find and thought it best to discover the situation without the girls present. The silence was deafening and not having at least Sally the poodle yipping was a daunting sign. Something was very wrong.

Once she was down on the ground, her frozen feet stung with pain as she took each step on the crunchy frozen lawn. Sloane quickly and cautiously circled around to the back entrance of their home and found the back door unlocked and opened more than a few inches. The odd smell hit her again and made her cough. What she saw inside, when she flashed her light beam around, made her sick. Not only were their supplies missing, but they also destroyed everything else that was left. Sloane took a step and stifled a scream from a sharp pain in her foot after having stepped on a large shard of broken glass.

She had to set her bag of supplies down to flash the light beam onto her foot. Blood streamed downward to the rice and dried beans strewn across the floor and as she reached for the glass piece, she realized it was imbedded deeply into the underside of her foot. "Ugh, that's just great." She pulled it out quickly and reached for the opened door that contained several dishtowels hanging out haphazardly.

"I'm such an idiot," she whispered to herself. It was one of those moments when all the hard work meant nothing and defeat meant everything. "Keep it together, girl," she told herself and took a deep breath. She couldn't afford the self-doubt now and wrapped her bleeding foot in the towel and applied pressure to the open wound. While she held still, she looked around and saw straight out the opened front door. Dry goods littered the entire way. "They certainly didn't give a darn about wasting anything."

Finally, she remembered just behind the kitchen door there was a pair of green Hunter rubber boots. They used to be a fashion statement; now they were a necessity. She kept the towel wrapped around her foot and shoved her feet into them. That was as good as she could do for now. She had other priorities underway and after clearing her lungs with the outside air, she wrapped another dishtowel over her mouth. After making her way through the kitchen and then the living room, she felt fairly sure there were no other intruders inside the house nor was there any sound from Sally. Sloane turned around toward the kennel where Sally slept at night. She peered into the crate, seeing only her curly white fur as she lay on her side.

She detected no gunshot wounds; no blood remained to indicate injury. Taking a few more steps, Sloane knelt down and opened the kennel. She felt for the dog's pulse at her neck and it was gone utterly, along with the life she once held.

"Oh no!" Sloane stood up and turned toward the door. She'd dropped the makeshift mask and ran.

Her steps slid after she ran around to the side yard of the house and nearly fell down the dewy grass incline. When she reached the girls' hideout, she was almost too afraid to know. She pounded three times with her fist in the cadence they'd planned and she waited in bitter agony. "Oh God, please no."

When met with only silence, again she beat the side of the steel door frame. "Wren! Open the door! Mae! Nicole! Please open the door, it's Mom!"

Nothing.

An eternity passed and she pounded again and begged for the door to open or a sign of some kind. Then movement from up the small incline caught her attention. She drew her gun before she realized and found herself aiming at Ace.

"Hi boy! Come here," she called and he did but swayed on all fours. When he reached her, he collapsed and licked her hands sleepily. She felt all over him and there were no injuries to find. Then suddenly the metal door latch creaked open weakly. Sloane shoved it open the rest of the way and grabbed the first hand she saw. She found herself screaming at the sight within the safety chamber, "Oh my God, no!"

23

Resolve

AS THE FIRST RAYS OF DAWN APPROACHED GLEAMING THROUGH the dark pines, Sloane found herself digging graves once again. The weather at first threatened to freeze her solid and now sweat dripped from her nose and mixed with dirt nearly too frozen to move with a shovel.

If she had to admit it, she cried too. Her arms ached as she reached down and lifted yet another shovel full of dirt and added it to the pile on the side. The hole was finally deep and wide enough and she wiped her face on her worn shirt sleeve. She couldn't remove the images from earlier. She'd reached inside and pulled Wren nearly unconscious from the gas that must have seeped and settled into the chamber from above. She'd coughed and hacked. Her eyes were swollen and then the other two girls—her younger daughter, Mae and her adopted daughter, Nicole—were motionless inside. "No!" Sloane leaped inside and pulled them both out of the gas-filled room. Neither breathed. It was torture to decide which one of them to perform mouth-to-mouth resuscitation on first. It might already be too late.

She'd listened for each heartbeat and began, hoping she'd made the right decision. Then she switched to the other and, in time, they'd both began to breathe.

"Mom!" Mae finally choked out when she was able.

Sloane cried—they all did—knowing that she'd nearly lost both girls, had she discovered them a few minutes later. She made them each breathe deeply despite the cold air burning their lungs. And instead of moving them inside the toxin-filled house, she put them into the neighbor's useless SUV to regain their strength and stuffed several warm blankets and pillows inside. Wren was weak but at least willed herself to open the door when her mother pounded.

"I'm sorry Mom, I didn't know what to do," Wren cried to her.

"It's okay, dove," Sloane assured her. "We made it. There're no easy answers now. Only the best one you can make at the time."

She'd patted and kissed her forehead before leaving them in the truck, along with Ace, who was slowly coming out of his brush with the gas as well.

She didn't tell them about Sally, nor what she was about to do. Instead, she went to each house containing her canine friends and found them all in still death. What she also found in each home was a canister of some kind of toxic gas.

Fury built in increasing volume with each discovery. In the end, it was only Ace that somehow made it out.

She'd spent the rest of the day checking on the girls and digging graves in intervals while she carted the bodies to the burial spot in the woods. Once the hole was big enough, she laid them out together, side by side, each with the buddy they liked the best. Her arms ached more than they ever did before, but she tossed in the dirt over each of them, thanking them for everything they'd done for her and the girls and hoping they went to a better life together.

Sloane went back to the truck and found the girls all awake as Wren gave them water to sip through their sore throats.

"Can we go inside now, Mom?" Mae asked shivering.

Sloane smiled at her girl and brushed her cheek with the back of her dirty hand, so thankful they were alive and yet so sad for what she was about to tell them.

"No, sweetheart. We can't. Listen," she said, "we have to make some big changes now. We can't stay here any longer. It's not safe."

"Where are we going?" Nicole asked.

Sloane took a deep breath. "First, I have to tell you something." The tears had already begun to flow despite her best intentions. "Like the gas you girls experienced in the chamber? All of the dogs were also gassed. Including Ace here, but he managed to get out of the house in time. The others...died."

She wasn't sure who broke down first but the only voice she heard was Wren's asking in dismay, "All of them?" And Sloane could only nod, too overcome to explain further.

She wiped away the tears, knowing they didn't have time for this. "We can't stay here. They know we're here. They'll come for us again. We have to leave now."

"Where are we going to go?" Wren nearly yelled.

Sloane didn't answer. "Where, Mom?" Wren yelled at her again, and this time the statement was more of a challenge.

"I don't know yet. I don't have all the answers, Wren, but we can't do this now. I know you're angry. And believe me, I'm angry too, but *this* was not my fault."

In return, Sloane received a hateful, hurt look from her daughter.

Sloane grabbed her daughter's hand. "We can't do this now. I almost wish we could. I wish things were that normal. They're not. I need your help now. Do you understand?" Sloane's eyes implored her daughter to get her meaning, to realize their very survival meant they must work together.

Wren's shoulders sagged finally and she began to cry while nodding her head. Sloane hated to see her girls unhappy, but she hoped this meant they at least were in a truce for the time being.

Sloane hugged her teenager, so like her father, and rubbed her back. "We have to get some things together. Can you help me?"

"Yes," Wren said and wiped her eyes.

"That's my girl. Let's buck up. We can't let them defeat us."

24

Gearing Up

After leaving Wren watching the younger girls, she quickly went through the ruined house and yanked out all the supplies left useful to them. Over time, she'd collected things from the other homes, like wagons, wheelbarrows and other useful items, and used them often to transport supplies from one end of the neighborhood to the other like a train. It wasn't a perfect method but it worked and kept them from breaking their backs with all the manual labor one woman and three girls could manage. Nicole had even devised a way to have the dogs pull the wagons, but now those days were, sadly, over. *At least*, Sloane thought, *we still have Ace*.

She cleaned herself up and changed out of her ruined flannel pajamas and into rugged gear, knowing the girls would need to do the same. She packed several layers of clothing and began hauling items out to the wagons and then went back to get the girls inside to dress for the day.

"Where are we going, Mom?" Mae asked as she ushered her inside the torn house. "What happened in here?" Mae's voice rose a decibel when she saw the devastation inside the house.

"Why did they do this?" Nicole asked.

Sloane let them take in the scene of destruction, of all their hard work. *Senseless* was the only way to describe it. "C'est la vie. It doesn't matter *why,* girls. It's done. Quickly, get cleaned up and changed. It's going to be a long night."

As the younger girls were doing as they were told, Ace remained by the open doorway and waited with Wren.

"*Why* did they do this, Mom?"

Sloane shook her head. "Control...they're trying to force us to their camp."

"Why don't we just go there then? It sounds like it would be better than this."

Turning to her daughter, Sloane said, "That's just it, dear. That's the way they make it sound so that you'll go along. Give up all of your rights and soon you're not a refugee, you're a prisoner and at their will and whim. No, I'm not submitting my children to that as long as I can help it. That's not survival, Wren, that's submission. Promise me you'll never give in."

Wren only nodded.

"Good girl. Tonight, we're staying at the house near the entrance to the neighborhood, Old Mr. and Mrs. Bishop's house. Then in the morning, we're leaving through the forest."

"It's cold at night, Mom."

"I know. We've started fires. We have tents. We'll keep moving until we find somewhere safe to go." One glance at her daughter told her she was terrified by the idea.

"We're no better off than those people who travel through here, are we?"

Sloane thought about her daughter's words then shook her head, "No dear, we're not; we never have been and we're in even more danger than that. But look at me, Wren, be brave in this world above all else. You must be brave."

She nodded and then Sloane led her girls, each with a filled backpack and pulling a wagon apiece, as they walked through the neighborhood until they reached the Bishops' house that backed up to the graveyard behind their house. Beyond the graveyard awaited the dark, cold, desiccating woods and the unknown.

25

Memories

Dark descended early that night. Every creep and sound made them jump. Even Ace was startled by more noises than usual. With only lantern light, they sat on sleeping bags on the den floor of what used to be a very nice home, but was now only a bleak reminder of what remained from better days.

"Mom, it's freezing in here. Can we light a fire in the fireplace?"

Sloane shook her head. "Too risky. We can't. They might be watching us. We can't take the chance of putting off a heat signal."

"You think they're watching us?" Nicole asked.

She nodded. "Yes, they were watching us before and they knew which house we were staying in and knew there were only four of us."

"So we didn't trick them this time?" Mae asked.

Sloane smiled. "No sweetheart, we didn't." Then Mae coughed

and Nicole followed suit. Sloane was concerned what damage the gas had on their respiratory systems. She was afraid they would have a lingering effect for days if not weeks, and if they were to catch a cold in the conditions she was forcing them into, it would further weaken their immune systems in time. "You two need to drink more water and catch some sleep, okay. We're getting up early in the morning to start on our journey." She opened Nicole's sleeping bag and helped her snuggle down.

"Sloane," Nicole whispered in a voice meek enough for the other two girls not to hear her, "is it okay that I'm...coming *with* you?"

Sloane finished tucking the girl in but her statement caused her to pause. Nicole's eyes were round and glossy. This child, now an orphan, had endured too much. Her concern nearly broke Sloane's heart.

"My dear, you are one of mine now. Of course you're coming; I'd never leave you behind."

Nicole's eyes stared into hers, looking for what Sloane thought was evidence of her conviction. She hoped beyond words that the girl found the solace she sought there.

Sloane bent down and kissed her forehead lightly. "I love you, Nicole, just like my own. Now please get some sleep."

Nicole nodded and turned to her side, closing her eyes.

"Mom, you should sleep now too; you were up all night. I'll keep watch," Wren said.

"I will, but not yet. I have a few things to do still. I'll leave Ace here with you. Try to stay awake and Wren, if anything happens, sound the alarm."

"Yes Mom."

Sloane stood and zipped up her black jacket and pulled on a black knit hat over her brunette hair. She donned her rifle and slung on her backpack.

"What are you going to do, Mom?" Wren whispered, trying not to disturb the younger girls trying to sleep.

Sloane knelt down. "I'm concerned they're going to show up again tonight, so I'm going to set up the contingency we talked about, to give us some time to get away if we need to. I want the girls to rest tonight after what happened this morning. I wish we had another day or two but we don't. They're coming back. So I'm going to make it very difficult for them to follow us."

"You might kill someone."

"Yes, I might. Especially if they are willing to try and harm us like they did today, I'd say they deserve it."

"But you're not them, Mom."

Sloane hated conversations like this. "Yes, it's them or us now, dove," she said and slipped away into the night back the way she came without engaging in another ethics debate with her idealistic daughter. That was a luxury of times past.

Months earlier, after they'd scavenged useful items from the abandoned homes, like car batteries, propane tanks and random ammunition or anything that wasn't adversely affected, they experimented with setting simple explosions. Wren seemed to retain all scientific information like her father had. So they pored over the science manuals he had stored in plastic totes that luckily survived the flood, and she and Wren began running experiments for other possible uses in defense. It was a great use of their down time. What they found was that while you always saw car batteries exploding easily in the movies, it was not so in their experiments and the explosions were easily the tamest, only the size of a closet. Not the worthiest weapon they could summon; however, some of the blue tipped ammunition they'd found in the Millers' house fit perfectly in the AR-10 she'd scavenged from the Carsons' home. She'd wondered why they were tipped in blue and when she tried a round, aiming at a concrete retaining wall, it not only hit the wall; it exploded on impact. She supposed these were incendiary rounds and they were supposed to be illegal in some states but perhaps Oregon wasn't one of them.

As Sloane walked out into the night, she began taking steps back toward her old home. She'd worked so hard to make them look lived in the past several months, in order to convince anyone who entered the neighborhood that it wasn't just her and the girls living here alone. Part of her knew her charade was only a temporary solution.

Now, as she passed each home, she remembered the families that once made their lives here, imagining them waving or playing in their yards as she walked by. Those same people were either dead now, living in a FEMA camp, surviving at a remote location, taken by the pandemic four years ago or from the tsunami wave of water that hit or the various other circumstances surrounding a crumbling society. It was devastating to know she and her girls were the only ones left in the neighborhood and now they too had to go on the run. Each home now sat empty as a cold monument to their deaths and in turn, as Sloane came to her own home and stood outside of it, it would be the same after tonight. Her breath puffed out in front of her as a chill ran through her bones. *No time to be weak. I won't let them just come in and take it all away without a cost*, she told herself and headed inside. It would be a long night of preparation.

Although the explosions wouldn't destroy everything, she aimed to do as much harm as possible. If placed prudently as a catalyst, the propane tanks would do a good amount of damage and that was the effect Sloane was going for when she began pulling the collected propane tanks from her basement to place in several of the homes. In particular, she placed the first full tank on an end table in the living room of the Carsons' house, right in front of the opened window in clear view. Then she placed a plastic bag filled with gasoline atop the tank. Afterwards, she closed up the house and then pulled the kitchen stove out from against the wall, making a horrible screeching racket by manhandling the door. She pulled a crescent wrench from her back pocket and opened the gas valve and then carefully left the house.

It would take hours for the unpredictable gas, leaking from the open valve, to fill the void. She hoped she had enough time. She repeated this procedure in her own home and several others. By now, she figured the neighbors who'd escaped were no longer coming home. She wanted to leave nothing behind for anyone else to take.

It was a long night of preparations and she hoped it was enough to give her and her girls enough time to escape into the woods when the time came.

When Sloane finished, she was spent of all energy, filthy and so exhausted she could only imagine the ghosts of those families saying goodbye to her as she passed again, one final time, back the way she came to their last shelter on Horseshoe Lane.

When she crept inside the house, only Ace was witness to her return. She heard the low growl until he knew it was her and then his head landed back into its position on his paws, relieved. Thankfully, Wren had fallen asleep as well. She couldn't take her daughter's brooding looks at the moment.

Sloane wiped the back of her hand over her tired eyes. She shuffled to the bathroom and used the lantern and a bottle of water they put there to wash by. By the glowing light, she found blood smeared across her face. She washed her hands as best she could, letting some of the water drain down the sink. Then she dampened a towel and cleaned her face. Though they'd learned to go days without a shower, Sloane couldn't get past at least cleaning this day's stench from her face and hands. The gas smell lingered on her hands even still.

After examining her hand more closely in the dim light, she'd found the source of the blood in a cut on the back of her wrist, though the blood had mostly subsided by now and it wasn't deep. She hadn't even known about the injury and it didn't matter now. While holding pressure on the wound with the damp rag, she stared at herself in the mirror in her weakened state, all the lines of a lady and mother, wife and daughter over forty reflected back to her. They were there, but so was the hardness that comes with trauma, an advance in aging since the last time she really looked at her reflection suddenly appeared. What else she saw there besides the lines were doubt and fear...*You can do this Sloane, you have to do this.*

She didn't want to leave Horseshoe Lane. Her husband was here. All the memories of her early happy life happened on this road in the house she'd just left behind. It was their first home as husband and wife. He'd carried her over the threshold there. It was where they brought their daughters home after bringing them into the world. It's where they fought, made love, and where she still felt him tinkering in the garage with one project or another. She felt him there with her still, whispering to her all the things she must do. It's why she hadn't left before when she knew she probably should have taken the girls and run. But she had to go now. She had to take the girls and run, not for her survival but for theirs, because she wanted nothing more than to die there in her home where her best, and despite the worst, her happiest memories remained.

Sloane rarely allowed herself to cry but she silently let the tears roll down her cheeks then. "I miss you," she whispered in case he heard her still.

26

No Rest

"Sloane," Nicole whispered.

Sloane slowly opened her eyelids to dim morning light, feeling as if they were peeling over asphalt, noting immediately that she felt dehydrated and needed water. Her mouth was gummy and she could only imagine how bad her breath was at the moment.

"What is it, dear?"

"We...hear...voices," Nicole's words came slowly and in an almost inaudible tone.

Sloane looked to her and then her eyes glanced at both of the other girls staring at her with alarm. Then she listened too because so far, she hadn't detected any noise. More curiously, Ace wasn't in the room, nor did she hear him anywhere.

She mouthed, "Ace?"

Nicole shook her head as if she didn't know.

Then she heard a vehicle's brakes squeak in the distance.

"Have you seen anyone?" she asked Nicole, whose face was still plastered into her sleeping bag.

"No," Nicole said.

There was no time to waste. Sloane pushed up on her elbows to her feet and then carefully peeked around the corner to where the noise was coming from through the front bay window of the house. She saw two Humvees out front through the dirty lace curtains. A few men with rifles in uniform were running in and out of the Carsons' home, only three houses down from where they were now.

Surely they must have already searched our old house?

She turned back to the girls, motioning them to hurry. She threw on her boots and grabbed her backpack and weapon and then grabbed Nicole and dragged them to the back door.

"What about the sleeping bag and the wagon?" Mae asked.

"Laisse le! Leave them. We don't have time. Allez, allez, let's go!" With only enough time to put on their shoes and grab their backpacks, Sloane checked the back yard finding no one there yet, and hand in hand they ran to the wooded area behind the house. Somewhere in her mind, she noted thankfully that it was a gray rainy day, providing them with more cover.

Once the four of them were in the forest, she checked to see if Wren followed close behind and found her looking back.

"Allez! Don't look back."

"What about Ace? Don't you care about him?"

Sloane grabbed her and pushed her forward. "Move! And keep down. Keep going! Don't stop until you get to Couthers Farm Road. Wait for me there. Stay hidden. Remember the plan, Wren."

Her daughter shot her an annoyed expression but nodded her head.

Sloane watched them disappear into the thicket until she heard voices getting closer behind her. She turned and headed back alone.

When she came to area where she buried the dead, she knew she was in range. She crouched down and pulled the AR-10, already loaded with the blue tipped incendiary .308 rounds, from the sling around her shoulder. She knelt behind the wood stump she'd practiced from before. Its girth was large enough to give her cover and high enough to brace against for a steadier shot. She got into position, tuned out all noise from her hearing, and glassed the area through the scope. She'd practiced this many times but her hands shook nonetheless. Just as a soldier was about to enter the Carsons' gas-filled home, she sighted the propane tank in the living room window, sucked in a short breath, let it out and pulled the trigger.

The yellow-white flash knocked her backwards. She was momentarily stunned. The AR-10, she found, had fallen to the side. The soldiers were running everywhere, not knowing what mayhem had fallen upon them. Suddenly, the Bakers' house exploded before she'd even sighted her next target. It must have caught automatically. She again set up her target, sucked in another quick breath, let it out and pulled the trigger, though this time her ears rang and there was no need to push out extraneous noises; she could hear nothing but the ringing in her head. After another blast, Sloane sighted her own home and the tank sitting in her bedroom window. She wasn't going to let them have anything; nothing of value would transfer into their hands. Yet a sudden lump formed in her throat. Another shot. As if in slow motion, she flashed on her husband Finn and cringed, waiting for impact. And just when the thought crossed her mind that perhaps she'd missed, the explosion shook the ground, causing her to fall backwards once again. She wasted no time shooting twice more in succession and by the time she was through, the street was engulfed in flames and she backed away quietly, without them knowing it was merely her.

Before she could escape, though, another burst went off and knocked her to her knees. She looked back. Men screamed as debris flew through the air. Somewhere in her mind, she knew the explosions would only get closer to her current position.

Sloane scrambled to her feet on the muddy ground and turned to run through the woods as fast as she could to catch up with the girls somewhere ahead of her, praying at the same time that they followed the plan safely.

Behind her, the flames grew and what once was a sanctuary to them, she'd destroyed so that they might flee and live another day.

27

A Home

After a while, the foliage became a blur. Her face and hands were scratched all over from carelessly running through the wet thicket in order to get to her children she already feared were lost to her.

Her legs burned and besides being soaking wet while running from mayhem, somewhere in her mind she worried about Ace, and the fact that she might be having a nervous breakdown while trying to hide herself and her children.

Then finally her eyes detected a flash of pink ahead through the forest and she began to slow her pace, taking care not to attract attention or scare the armed girls unnecessarily.

She came to the waiting spot and found them huddled together underneath several bushes hiding and, she suspected, trying to take cover from the rain.

"Mom!" Mae yelled and jumped up when she spotted her mother.

"Shhh! It's okay. I'm here now," she said.

"I'm so scared. Did you hear all of that? What's happening?" Mae asked frightened.

"Yes, Mae. Keep quiet," she said to her terrified daughter but ignored her questions and then her eyes swept over the other two terrified girls. "We can't stay here. We have to keep moving."

Then she remembered the pink jacket that caught her attention earlier and though her lungs burned she quickly told her daughter, "Wren, peel off your jacket and turn it inside out. Allez! Do it now; it's too bright."

Wren looked at her like she was crazy but complied even though she had to put the wet side against her clothing and let the gray interior get soaking wet.

"Let's go," she told them. "We have to find shelter before nightfall."

Always preferring solid plans, this was the part that she'd dreaded. She had no real idea what was out there beyond Horseshoe Lane. The farthest she'd ever imagined was the house she was headed to at the end of the woods, hoping that those who came for them thought they'd left long ago and didn't have a clue where they'd gone.

The high school where she'd taught French seemed a different life and at first, she had planned to possibly go there, but realized in all their training, it was more than likely being used as a holding facility for what they were now calling Americans...*refugees*. At least that was what the initial notices said when they received them after the flood that displaced so many.

She continued to push the girls forward through the brush. The conifers were gaining in height the farther they ventured and the brush denser in this part of the woods, and she knew they were headed in the right direction. Her fear beyond being caught was possibly running into more stragglers out in the woods. It seemed a natural hiding place to get out of sight from the old open farmland where their homes were built.

"Mom, where are we going?" Wren, who was in the lead, asked as she pushed branches out of her way.

"Continue heading northeast. We'll be there by tonight. We can stop and rest in a while, but let's get farther away still," Sloane said, raising her voice an octave above a whisper to counter the increasing rainfall.

"I'm cold," Mae said with her teeth chattering.

"I know, me too, but we can't stop now," Sloane said.

"Where *are* we going?" Nicole asked.

Sloane expected complaining about the cold, wind and rain. What she dreaded were the questions about their direction and where they might possibly be spending the night. In truth, there was only one place she thought they might be able to hide for a time, and it was a place the girls would not want to go.

She and Finn found it while hiking these woods when Wren was only a three-year-old swinging between their arms as they went. They'd came through the opening in the woods and found a house in a clearing surrounded by trees with only one driveway leading out. The house was an enchanting old model with overgrown rose bushes and hedges showing little care, though Sloane could see the remnants of a once glorious estate. They'd explored the grounds before they found someone watching them. A kind old man sat staring at them from a rocking chair on the weathered porch.

Sloane was startled. Finn wore a navy blue windbreaker that day. He'd grabbed her arm just above her elbow to steady her, sensing she was about to flee. "Hi there." He'd waved to the older gentleman and they approached the porch.

"What are you folks doing here?" the elderly man had labored to say.

"I apologize for trespassing. We were just hiking through the woods and came upon your place here. We live a few miles that away, as the crow flies," Finn pointed into the trees.

The old man had nodded, his eyes blue and rheumy. Sloane

watched as his gaze traveled down to Wren. Her little hand clutched hers tighter when he smiled and showed little teeth.

"No harm done. You folks are welcome here," he said and then looked into Sloane's eyes. At the time, she felt like he stared straight to her soul. There was something about the man that gave her chilling goosebumps and she chided her inner self for her anxiety. He'd given her a smile like he gave Wren and she smiled back at him, hoping his interrogation of them was over with. That's what it felt like. He measured them like a laser beam detecting ore. He scanned them for something, offering a smile at the end of his service.

Sloane had never had elderly grandparents to compare him with. She assumed old people came with different rules and guidelines for social graces. This old man surely did.

"Well, we'll be off then. Sorry to disturb your afternoon here," Finn had said kindly.

They'd turned to leave and then Sloane heard, "You, what's *your* name?" She'd thought he was talking to Finn but, when she turned to look at him, found he was addressing her.

"Sloane, Sloane McKenna," she said. "And your name is?" she asked in return, to be polite.

The question stagnated for a time. It occurred to her that he might be hard of hearing, which was a likely scenario, when suddenly he said, "I'm Garrison. Wayne Garrison."

She smiled again. "Well, it's nice to meet you, Mr. Garrison."

"We should go if we want to make it back before dark," Finn suggested and they waved goodbye again and turned up the long driveway that seemed to lead to the main road. Halfway up the drive Sloane felt the old man's eyes on them still and when she turned to look, the rocking chair stood empty. She hadn't heard the man get up or enter the home and thought it odd at the time.

Weeks later, Finn ran to the hardware store in search of a certain size washer and came home after his errand white as a sheet. When she asked what was wrong, he said he'd mentioned old Wayne Garrison's name, who lived at the beautiful estate, and the old clerk said he'd died ten years earlier.

The home was abandoned and a distant cousin said she'd never sell the place because she thought he haunted the grounds he used to lovingly maintain for his departed wife. She'd laughed then, thinking he was joking with her, but he shivered like he was totally creeped out and for a man of science, she kidded him about it for a time.

"It was probably a neighbor checking in on the place or something, right? Had to be," he'd reasoned.

They'd never returned there even when she teased him and asked him if he was the least bit curious. Finn was always skittish when it came to things he couldn't explain. It would weigh on his mind and it was something she loved about him. There always had to be a plausible explanation but this time, nothing came.

The thing was, Wren remembered the encounter too, even as small as she was. She remembered the old man and the house and asked her mother about it after the incident a few nights in a row when she was saying goodnight in the quiet of her room, whispered like an anomaly. "Who was that old man, Mom?" or "The house was scary," she shared with toddler eyes round in wonder. So much like her father, Wren was. Always needing exact instructions or explanations for the things she didn't fully grasp.

Sloane knew her daughter already suspected their destination and she expected a coming battle over it but Sloane could think of no better place to hide for at least the next day or two. Surely the abandoned house would be a safe haven until she could figure out where to go from there.

"Mooom?" Wren had stopped in the lead and turned to her with a question. "We're going to the old house, aren't we?"

Sloane nodded as the rain pelted them, their eyes blinking in defiance. Nicole shivered with Mae in their soaked gear between them, looking from one of them to the other. It was a standoff in a sense. Wren was a smart girl; surely she could see they had few options? Sloane watched her daughter's expression. It saddened her but the last few years had matured the girl beyond her years. She looked at her siblings in the rain, cold and shivering. Then only a curt nod was necessary. Wren cut her eyes down and forged ahead.

Sloane's heart broke right there in front of her eyes. Her daughter, seeing their circumstances, had become an adult. She'd overcome her fears out of necessity, knowing they needed shelter and the scary house of her childhood was the only option despite that fear.

They forged through the increasing rain, her daughter leading and Sloane ushering them from behind. Then, soaking wet with her long brown hair plastered against her alabaster skin, Wren turned to her mother asking for directions, only the wind had picked up so much she barely heard her words only four feet ahead of her. Sloane looked up at the swaying trees. Even the forest was becoming unsafe for them now. Sloane shuffled ahead of them, past the other two girls, and took Wren by the arm and pulled the other two close into a circle. She had to yell to be heard, even that close. "Hold on to each other. I'll lead. Don't let go." They all nodded since there was no use wasting their voices. With Sloane holding Nicole's hand in hers and Mae holding onto to Nicole, Wren pulled up the end holding her sister Mae's hand. The wind was so strong they leaned into it regardless of the stinging rain and guarded their faces with their arms.

Sloane wasn't sure of the exact location of the house but knew it couldn't be much farther. Time seemed to hold no meaning. It felt like ages since the morning raid, and night seemed to dally rather than arrive. *It would be my luck to escape into a storm*, she thought. Then one of the girls screamed the words, or she thought it was one of them. When she looked, it was Mae, who'd wrenched her arm away from Nicole and yelled repeatedly while pointing through the trees, "Mom! There!" She jumped up and down, repeating the words over and over. Sloane looked and saw the camo greenish tone of something solid in a clearing up ahead. She nodded behind her and went farther still. When they arrived at the edge of the clearing where wild grasses swayed as the air currently played over them like some madman doodling on parchment, one glance at the house and she knew this was it.

Though time had taken its toll, the hidden two-story Victorian house that time forgot was still in an upright position and seemed intact. She crouched at the back edge of the property and had the girls do the same. She needed to study the place in hopes no one was in residence or harboring safely within its walls. The back porch faced her view. A once fully enclosed porch, the now-brittle rusted screens hung in peeled suspension at random intervals though most voids were not as graceful, showing ragged abrupt breaks. She imagined if she attempted to right the material, it would fall apart in her hands, staining them orange.

"Mom, can we go in?" urged Mae, drenched and kneeling beside her in the sloppy brown mud. With no one in sight across the overgrown lawn, only the dark and disintegrating porch greeted them from this angle.

"Yes, but follow me closely. Wren, keep your weapon ready."

"Yes Mom," she said and they paced quickly through the sheeting rain, aiming in a cautious line for the back entrance.

Sloane tested the first step of the worn wooden porch, just knowing her foot would fall right through the weathered wood. She pushed her weight onto it and hefted herself up. Surprisingly, the stairs were solid though slick, like a log not used to wear. "Be careful, it's slippery," she cautioned. She opened the first partially screened door and ushered them inside.

Just being out of the rain with a tin roof overhead felt better. Then Sloane approached the darkened back door. It was painted over more than once, the color of damp moss with a glass paned window. A curtain kept her vision limited on the other side. She reached for the brass knob.

"Shouldn't we knock first?" Mae said.

"It's abandoned," she said.

"How do we know for sure?" Wren asked.

Still the rain continued its assault, and she barely heard their reasonable objections. She knocked, or rather pounded, on the side of the glass. "Anyone home?"

They waited a time. Sloane looked around the empty porch. No debris or signs of anyone living there. If anything, it looked a bit too clean.

"See, no one's here," she said and before she or any of the girls could talk her out of it she tried the knob, cold in her already chilled hand, as she turned and found it locked.

Okay, what now?

"Why don't we try the front door? Maybe they can't hear us. It's so loud out here," Nicole advised.

Sloane agreed and led them to the front, cautious of any signs someone was lurking there waiting to catch them.

Without the trees to shield them, the rain felt like stinging needles coming at them in a sideways assault. They hurried to the front, where Sloane halted at the corner. She stepped into the garden bed and peeked around the sharp corner of the house. Like the back, no one lingered outside. No cars were parked in the long dirt drive. Sloane shielded her eyes from the storm and realized even the drive itself was overgrown. She could barely make out where the entrance through the trees began. "There's no one here," she said to the shivering girls.

Satisfied, Wren asked, "How do we get inside?"

Sloane quickly led them the return trip to the secluded porch. She reasoned a broken pane would be less noticeable in the back window than in the front of the house.

The girls stood around her as she removed her backpack first, and then her own jacket. She wrapped it around her left hand.

"What are you doing?" Mae asked.

"Mom's breaking into the house," Wren explained.

Sloane gave her a look.

"What? That's what you're doing isn't it?" Wren asked.

Huffing, Sloane looked at the girls. "I'm going to break this pane of glass and then reach in and unlock the door," Sloane explained.

"That's wrong," Mae said.

Wren must have taken pity on her mother because she intervened with, "Mae, we have to get into this house. We have no place else to go and this house is abandoned. The bad guys won't find us here."

Mae nodded as she and Nicole shivered, still aware of the increasing storm. "Well, hurry up, please," Mae urged. And with that, Sloane punched the glass pane nearest the door's knob. Unfortunately, the glass didn't break but Sloane was beginning to think her hand was broken as shooting pains ran up to her elbow.

"Ow! Gosh, that hurt!" Sloane shouted while shoving her hand between her legs. She bent over, unwrapped her hand and examined her red knuckles.

"Here, let me try," Wren insisted. "You have to aim for the other side of the glass, just like in Tae Kwon Do," she said as she too wrapped the jacket around her hand.

Still holding her own hand Sloane said, "No Wren, wait," but it was too late. Wren punched through the glass pane, causing a loud shattering. They all ducked at the sound and waited for the result they feared, but no one came running toward them. No alarm was sounded and as far as they could tell, they were the only ones to hear the breaking glass. Hoping the sound was disguised by the heavy winds, Sloane looked at her daughter. "Where did you learn to do that?"

Wren raised her shoulders. "I don't know. Dad taught me."

Sloane sent a silent prayer, along with a thank you, to her deceased husband. Before they could make any more noise, Sloane put her uninjured hand through the broken glass pane and reached for the deadbolt lock. She unlocked the door after staring inside what she decided was the old kitchen for a while. Then she opened the door. Again broken glass made a racket but she was fairly certain the noise was absorbed by the outside storm. After pushing the door inside, she took a few tentative steps within the house with glass crunching underneath her boots. She made the girls come just inside the entranceway and closed the door behind them. She stood there in front of the girls in the dim kitchen. The solid wide plank flooring echoed a history of caring, toil, family, and scars of those left behind. White painted cabinets contrasted with the dark flooring with their black hammered cast iron hinges and door pulls. The storm still raged beyond the white framed windows; shadows of branches swung back and forth through the simple white curtains drawn closed, casting scary shadowed images onto painted pale blue walls. In the center of the large space, an old brown stately table sat with four upholstered chairs mounded with a thick layer of dust; beyond that was a typical large fireplace that was the mainstay of homes this old for cooking everything before the age of the modern appliances took hold. She'd always wanted a house like this; it was a dream home. And it was obvious someone once loved it very much by the looks of the kitchen alone.

"Stay here," she whispered to them. "Let me check it out first," she cautioned. Sloane left her backpack with the girls and unholstered her Glock, keeping it out for her own protection. She glanced back at the girls, still shivering and dripping water onto the old plank floor, forming puddles around their boots as they stood there frightened, cold and drenched. She had a momentary thought of tossing them a towel to keep the floor from harm but it passed out of necessity. There wasn't time for that now.

Sloane's boots squeaked as she stepped through the dim kitchen to a short dark wainscoted trimmed doorway leading to what she could see from the opened doorway was the dining room. If the shadows warring on the kitchen walls hadn't scared her, the ones racing on the formal dining room certain did. This room too was covered in a thick layer of dust. The same wide plank flooring existed but also an old ornate rug sat under the heavy feet of a large handsome dining table with six chairs surrounding it and silver period candle sticks atop. Sloane avoided stepping on the rug with her wet boots but passed an old buffet table with a gold framed portrait over the top. She guessed the beach scene painting was of Haystack Rock; every home had some similar rendition. The gold frame set off the eggshell blue painted walls. The one thing different about this room was the raw hewn beams traversing the ceiling, causing her to question if she'd literally stepped back in time. It certainly felt to her like living in the 1800s. Another fireplace with a white painted wood mantle sat adjacent the table and Sloane wanted nothing more than to light a fire in it while she and girls gathered around it for warmth. But first she needed to check out the rest of the house.

Sloane stepped again across the hallway leading to the front door and found herself in a red painted room with the same flooring. It looked like a formal sitting room, smaller than the dining room. Again, another white painted wood fireplace lined one wall. Large rough beams traversed the ceiling. A dusty writing desk sat along one wall and next to the windows were two chairs flanking an end table. A few other chairs were scattered about some with brocade pillows atop them so dusty she couldn't tell their color. Several gold framed portraits lined the walls; she glanced at them wondering if these people haunted these walls, if they minded her presence here or not. She couldn't tell yet. She needed to be here. She needed this sanctuary and she hoped they understood—that is, if there was a consciousness to this house at all.

She came to a white door and turned the black cast iron knob in her hand, not knowing where it might lead. Expecting the old man from years before to appear around every corner, she kept suppressing her fears. "Get a grip, Sloane," she whispered to herself.

On the other side, she found a smaller room. Same flooring but white walls this time. Two gold framed portraits hung on one wall; the difference was this room was lined with bookshelves from floor to ceiling on three sides. One grand table sat in the middle with a wood chair on either side. Two ornate upholstered chairs sat in corners. A long, tall window draped in velvet curtains stood in the center. Sloane's nose began to tingle. She was afraid she was going to sneeze any minute, knowing the dust was getting to her senses.

"Mom?" called Wren's voice.

Sloane waited to answer while she stood stock-still listening for any sound that didn't belong. Any creaking along the now-familiar flooring that wasn't coming from the kitchen or from her. She heard no movement and then answered, "I'm fine, just wait there still." She knew they were worried but she needed to continue searching. Of course, now their cover was blown but no one within the house had reacted to the noise, at least not yet.

She retreated from the library and stepped back into the red sitting room, then headed for the hallway once again. After peeking out the front she spied the dilapidated rocking chair she'd met Garrison sitting in years ago. A shiver ran down her spine as she remembered the man and now she was inside his house, hoping he didn't still haunt the walls or at least hoping he didn't mind them being here if he did.

She turned down the hallway, still with her boots squeaking on the floor. A staircase sat in the center of the large hallway, beautifully carved and graceful in its lines as it wound upward to the second floor. She could only imagine the bedrooms above for now. She continued past the staircase and found a room she'd missed after the staircase. This room, a delight beyond the next, continued the wide plank flooring, this time with walls painted gray with the same white trim detailing as the others. Several windows lined two walls, two along the wall leading to the backyard and another showing the side of the property. Again, another fireplace lined the farthest wall, as ornately carved as the others if not more. A landscape painting trimmed in gold hung above it and a grand piano sat in a corner. As in the library, heavy red velvet drapes hung from floor to ceiling windows. A baroque settee sat on side on one side of her; an oriental rug flanked by two matching chairs and a roughhewed coffee table remained in the center of the room. Various artifacts lay on the mantle and the built-in shelves. She opened a side door off of this room and found a bathroom painted the same gray as before. *This is a house you could get lost in.* The one thing she was thankful for was that there were no signs of any use for quite some time. Even her footprints left marks on the dusty flooring, indicating no one had stepped there since the layer landed over years past.

After leaving the gray room she headed across the hallway to the kitchen where the girls where now squatting and shivering in a huddle by the doorway.

"I know it's cold. I still need to check upstairs. If it checks out, we'll start a fire and warm up one of the rooms." With quivering chins, the girls nodded assent and Sloane turned back down the hallway heading for the darkly carved staircase.

Something in her stomach tightened when she took the first step. The air thickened around her. More than a tingle went up her spine this time. She suddenly wanted to flee. With her hand on the banister, she took her second step on the rug-lined stairs. She hated to leave the dusty marks with her footsteps but she could think of no other way. As her hand graced the banister railing, dust accumulated like a train. Gray dust bunnies gathered on the back of her hand and she suddenly thought of mites and shook off the debris. She watched it slowly sink onto floor below. *This house seriously needs a good dusting,* she thought then she sneezed loudly three times.

If there had been a murderer upstairs he surely waited for her now, knowing her exact position.

Sloane continued up the stairs, determined to shake off both the scaredy-cat she'd become and the dust allergy she knew pervaded her senses.

A hallway teed at the top of the stairs with a Tiffany lamp sitting on a side table next to a red upholstered chair. A decades-old phone hung on a wall above it. She couldn't guess what century the phone was from; she'd never seen anything like it. A stained-glass window barely lit the area with a soft multicolored glow coming from the beautiful rose design. There were five doors lining the dark hall. She first opened the one in the center and it led to a brightly lit gray bathroom. Again she tried to date the house or at least those that occupied it last. The toilet was the kind with the overhead tank; she couldn't remember the last time those were used. She had memories of seeing them as a girl in old buildings but had no real reference as to what decade they were from. A cast iron claw foot tub sat on one side and tile lined the sparse room. There was no shower head, only the tub and then a pedestal sink sat on the other side with a beautiful leaded glass mirror hung above it. She wasn't surprised to see a small fireplace in the bathroom at the far wall. Storage cabinets were painted white like the trim and window and recessed into the deep wall. The tiny white octagonal tiles, though dusty, showed no chips or wear. An oval window above the claw foot tub with spider leaded glass design was the only natural light in the room. "Hmmm."

She closed the door and decided to go left first, to the nearest door. She'd try the last door before the staircase on her way down.

The next door opened up to a bedroom with two twin wood framed canopy beds with matching whole cloth linen quilts flanking a large blue velvet-lined window. A tattered rug lay on the floor between them. And shadows struck odd angles on the walls with the dormered ceiling. There was barely any light and before she knew it, she walked into a spider web. She waved her injured hand through the air to get rid of the menace when she heard a noise from down the hall. She shamed herself immediately for becoming too comfortable, too lax and confident that no one was near. The girls were downstairs still; what would become of them if something happened to her?

She quickly backed out of the room and closed the door, standing silently, waiting for the next sound to make itself heard. Her breath shortened when the scratching began again. She thought of it as a scratching sound and imagined a boot dragging carefully across the wooden flooring. *But why would he risk the noise and not pick up his feet?* She thought.

She heard it again, sure it was someone lurking on the other side of the next door. "Hello?" she said but was met with silence. "I'm sorry to intrude. We just need a place to stay. We mean you no harm," she said when she heard it again. She swallowed hard, the back of her throat scratchy from the dust she'd inhaled.

She reached out for the black cast iron knob as before and noticed her hand shaking as she did. She was terrified and wanted nothing more than to flee down the stairs but that was a luxury she didn't have anymore. She had to face whatever was beyond the door. "I mean you no harm," she repeated as she took the handle firmly in her hand and turned it.

The door flung open, one of the girls screamed, "Mom!" and instantly she was torn but focused on what she saw in the room first. With her heart hammering in her chest she yelled downstairs, "Is everything all right?"

"Yes, are you okay? We heard you talking to someone."

She turned from the bedroom and went to the banister so that her voice would carry better. "I'm fine, Mae. It's fine. I heard a noise and thought there might be someone here but it turns out a tree branch has made its way into one of the bedrooms and was scratching on the window frame." Her breathing was still rapid and then suddenly she felt something brush up against her leg and she screamed loudly.

"Mom!" Mae cried.

Sloane turned around, weapon drawn, and expected someone

to be standing right behind her but found only the back end of a gray cat fleeing back into the bedroom, startled by her scream.

"Oh my gosh, I'm going to have heart attack here!" she said with her hand literally over her pounding heart. Mae continued to cry below in distraught heaves with her sister and Nicole shushing her.

"It's okay, Mae. It was only a cat. I scared it more than it scared me. Whew! I'll be down in a few minutes, girls. I'm sorry it's taking so long. There are a lot of rooms in this place."

"It's okay, Mom," Wren said. "We're fine."

Though she heard Mae still crying, she couldn't blame her daughter. Her own nerves were shot as well. With two more doors to check, she briefly considered leaving them an unknown. Instead, she continued on in a more hurried pace. She went to the damaged room that the cat fled back into and looked for the kitty. Seeing its eyes glowing at her from under the bed, she said, "Come here. I won't scream at you again."

The cat must have partly believed her; it scurried toward her and then beelined past her and down the hall to the stairs. She wasn't sure if it was a stray or if it belonged in the old house. It probably came through the broken window along with the tree branch swaying against the house. Before she closed the door, she looked at the ruined room. A part of the floral wallpaper was torn and falling on one side nearest the window. The curtains, which were once nice she assumed, were blackened with mold and were literally falling apart with rot. A queen bed was moved at an angle and not at all in the neat condition the rest of the house had followed. The floor was water damaged and all sorts of debris from past storms lay strewn all over the room. She imagined there was probably more than one critter taking refuge in the room and decided to close the door behind her.

She stepped farther down the hall and opened the next door; this one faced the front of the house. When she opened the door, she guessed it was the master bedroom. A large, dark wood four-poster queen bed sat over an enormous baroque rug in hues of murky gold. Needlepoint decorative pillows, though faded from the sun coming in from the opposite window, sat offering a guest respite still after all these years. Opposite the bed was another fireplace with dusty candles still sitting in brass candlesticks connected by spider webbing.

As she entered the room she walked almost reverently around the bed. *Someone loved this place once.* She reached out and straightened one of the dusty green candles that had angled over time. At the edge of the room stood a smaller door; she opened it and found a cedar-lined closet nestled into a dormer, still with belongings hung with care on wooden hangers. She reclosed the space smelling of moth balls and in front of the bed frame she found a yellow-painted pine trunk. *A blanket chest*, she thought. There were probably cleaner blankets in there instead of taking one from one of the dusty beds. She knelt down to open it and its hinges squeaked as she slowly lifted the top. Inside lay striped ticking blankets that probably hadn't been touched in decades or more; she was afraid to speculate. She reached inside and pulled out the top two bundles. They smelled of moth balls and cedar but at least the dust was less than in the room. She went to close the chest and found lying on top of another blanket several old envelopes and a beautiful bone-handled knife in a sheath. "I'll take only what I need," she said to anyone who might be listening and carefully replaced the trunk lid.

With one room to go, she closed this door behind her as she left and moved on to the last room in the hall. She opened this door and found another room with twin beds like the first. This time the color scheme was more feminine than the one before. Two beds with faded light pink spreads sat in the center of the room with two windows with white lacy curtains. One wall was complete with cupboards for storage and the other was centered with another fireplace. A homemade rag doll sat on the mantle along with a miniature tea set with pink roses on white china. She opened the small doors and found another cedar-lined closet, with a few dusty belongings of residents past. She didn't have time to check out the decade they might be from. Her mother's instincts kept telling her she needed to get downstairs to her girls. Finding no foes, she held the mothball-smelling blankets close and her gun a little more relaxed at her side as she exited the room and closed the door behind her. There was nothing to be afraid of upstairs or down. Then she wondered if the house had a basement. That would have to wait. Her girls had been through enough; it was time to get them warm and dry.

28

Kitty

ON THE WAY DOWN THE STAIRS, SHE NOTICED THE HALLWAY had darkened with the storm but also the time of day, which she met with both a blessing and in scary anticipation. She needed to get an inconspicuous fire going in one of the rooms on the main level and make the girls comfortable for the night. They had a few rations in their bags to eat, now she only debated which room was the least scary that she could have them comfortably lie down around a fireplace without their sleeping bags and other gear they had to leave behind.

She found them as before, huddled together on the puddled floor, Wren in front of the younger two girls with her weapon lying across her lap. They looked pale and beyond cold. The younger girls were still suffering from sore throats from the gas they'd inhaled and their pale skin worried her. She had no idea what effect those chemicals would have on them over time. She missed Ace, wishing he was there with them to help guard their safety, and she simply loved him and worried he'd died in the fire searching for them or was shot by the crazed government agents. Either way, she missed her furry friend. "Okay girls, come with me," she urged.

"Are we staying *here?*" Mae asked in a sort of horror that broke her heart.

"Yes, it's safe enough. There isn't anyone here. It's been abandoned for a long time now."

"It's creepy," Mae pouted.

"It'll be okay," Wren said in forced reassurance.

One look at her older daughter and Sloane knew she too was terrified of the house and its strange furnishings but she was coping.

"Come on," she said again and helped Nicole up from the floor. She was still damp and shivering. She led them into the gray room with the piano. At least in that room there was a separate door leading into the backyard, which gave them more than one exit if needed. Besides that, she suspected it was a family room at one time and it seemed a little less scary than the rest of the house.

"Where'd you get the blankets, Mom?" Wren asked.

"Upstairs in an old chest," she said.

"Everything's so dusty," Nicole remarked.

"Yes, this house was abandoned long ago, I suspect, but that's a good thing for us. It's secluded and I don't think many people know it's hidden back here, so we'll see how it goes for a few days. Did you guys see a cat?"

"No, what cat?" Nicole asked, her eyes round with wonder.

"The gray cat that made me scream earlier. It ran down the stairs. I thought it might have gone into the kitchen."

Wren shook her head, "No, we never saw a cat."

"Hmmm?" It hardly seemed possible since she remembered watching the scared feline run past her and down the staircase. *Where did he go?* She wondered.

The girls marveled at the gold-framed portraits against the gray walls as they followed her to the fireplace at the end of the long rectangular room.

"What is this place? Where they rich and famous?" Mae asked.

Sloane chuckled. "I don't think so. I think they probably kept a lot of their family heirlooms and passed them down the generations."

"Look at that old piano," Nicole said.

"Can I play it later, Mom?" Wren asked.

Sloane gave her a sad shake of the head. She would like nothing more than to let her girls run around and make themselves at home here but that wasn't their life now. Every second was precious and one of caution if they were going to survive this.

"No dear, sorry. We have to keep quiet. There are other buildings out here and a basement that I haven't checked yet. There could still be someone hiding out here. Drawing attention to ourselves is the last thing we need to do."

"I'm freezing, Mom," Mae reminded her, wrapping her arms around herself and shuddering.

Sloane looked at her daughter. Her voice still sounded hoarse and she looked as pale as ever. She ran her hand over her forehead, checking for warmth covertly as she embraced her and rubbed her arm. "Give me a few minutes to get a fire going."

"Mom," Wren said, "won't smoke coming out of a chimney attract attention too?"

Sloane took a deep breath in, regardless of the dusty air, and let it out. She'd thought of that. But the fact remained, she needed to get the girls warmed up fast. There was dry wood sitting at each fireplace in the house. She'd noticed that as she went through. They were secluded in the woods with an overgrown single driveway and hopefully, no one else around. Not only that, it was dusk and by the time she had the fire going, if the flue was clear, it would be dark and no one could see the smoke coming from the fireplace on a moonless night like tonight. With the house fires miles away, even the smell of smoke would be masked by the ones earlier in the day. "I think we'll take the risk considering it's nearly dark and we're pretty secluded in a big storm. We need to get warmed up before we get sick. You girls need to sleep. It's been a really long day."

That explanation seemed to be enough for Wren for now. Her daughter seemed satisfied and removed her backpack when they reached the fireplace. "How does it work?" Wren asked with reference to the cold open cavern.

"We've always had gas fireplaces, haven't we? This is old school. There's an art to building a good fire," Sloane said as she knelt down in front of the hearth.

"Can we use some of the couch cushions, Mom?" Wren asked as she began to make a comfortable area in front of the fireplace for them.

"Sure, first lay one of the blankets down on the floor. Then sit on top of that. Take a few cushions carefully over to the other side of the room and shake them out. Use the other side to lean against. We need to keep as much dust out of our lungs as possible."

Wren agreed and did as her mother asked while Sloane turned on her flashlight and shined it up into the chimney. She didn't relish sticking her hand in a dark hidden place filled with who knows what creepy crawlies hanging out by the old chimney. She really couldn't see much with the angle of the flue but assumed the damper was closed. She looked around the fireplace and found a brass hook hanging from a fireplace set with a carved pineapple on one end. Thankful she didn't have to use her hand after all, she reached in with the hook and guesstimated which direction it needed to go, either up or sliding sideways. In this case it gave way upwards but not before releasing a lot of debris and more than a few bugs down into the fireplace. "Ewww...great!" she said, knowing full well how silly she was being. This was survival now and a few spiders were the least of her worries.

Once the damper was set in place she looked around for what to use as kindling. She hadn't noticed it before but next to the neat dry stack of wood there was also a canister of small sticks, gray with age, standing in a crock cylinder right next to the wood. *Of course there is.*

She set out stacking a three-log design on the cast iron grate, the way Finn had taught her many years ago, and then underneath that she scattered piles of the dry kindling and knew the debris of pine needles that had fallen down from the damper would also work well to light the fire. She pulled her backpack to herself and though it was still damp from the rain, she knew just where to find the matches she'd previously packed that were both waterproof and wrapped in secure plastic bags. She lit the match and the girls all watched. The flame grew brighter as the kindling caught. It was now nearly pitch dark in the room with only a low blue cast through the window to see by. Soon, their eyes were mesmerized by the fire growing ever brighter and catching onto the seasoned logs easily.

She assessed the girls' condition. They still coughed intermittently and in a sequence that made her nervous. She began pulling out water bottles from their packs and an MRE each for them to eat.

Wren opened up the other blanket and laid it across their laps as the three girls relaxed against the old cushions propped up against their backpacks for support. The fire began to warm them as Sloane kept watch with her weapon by her side. She also drank her own bottle of water and an energy bar from her pack but surveyed the room and windows as the girls began to relax.

"After you eat, please try to sleep. I'll keep watch and feed the fire." They seemed comforted by her words though she wasn't comforted by the sound of the younger girls' voices. They coughed and hacked every few minutes; even Wren coughed a time or two, just not as much. *Damn those selfish men. Why couldn't they just leave us alone?*

It wasn't long before she noted their snores. She wasn't sure how they fell asleep so fast. She was just as scared of the eerie house as they were and couldn't imagine closing her eyes right now, no matter how tired she felt. Having the fire flames' reflection dance across the elegant gray walls didn't help either. She took another drink from her water bottle, slowly swallowing, letting the tepid liquid soothe her raw throat. *Maybe we could stay here...not long term but for the time being.*

Her glance hovered over Nicole now, whose eyelids she continued a lazy war with. She was failing slowly to keep them open and trained on Sloane. She'd noticed that Nicole did this before she slept. Perhaps she was afraid she and her girls would leave her and run off somewhere. Keeping her eyes on Sloane meant she couldn't go anywhere. *Not a chance, kiddo.*

With her Glock in her lap she continued to nibble her energy bar and watch her surroundings, guarding her children. Then her eye caught movement along the shadows of the wall—not only dancing flames but the silhouette of a cat coming her way as well. Her breath sucked in, as she tried to make sense of its direction. "Kitty?"

And then it stood at the edge of the couch, looking at her with its green eyes.

"Hey, where've you been?"

The gray cat rubbed against the dusty tapestry of the couch. "Come here, mister," she said, patting her leg.

The cat didn't hesitate; it soon slinked onto her lap without hesitation and curled up into a donut between her crossed legs. "Well, make yourself at home," she said.

As she petted the cat's long gray fur, the purring began almost immediately. "You're sure a strange guy. I thought you might be feral but you seem totally tame." His green eyes, in dreamy ecstasy, acknowledged her words momentarily. She glanced at her girls to see if their eyes were open and debated briefly whether or not to wake them, then priority won out and she let them sleep. There was time tomorrow for the cat to bring up their spirits.

As she pulled her fingers through his fur, there was hardly a snarl in his long mane, as if he'd been cared for daily. "You must be someone's house-cat. Let's see, no tags and you're not skinny. How did you get here? You must have come through the broken window but how did you get through the woods in such good condition?" He didn't give her an answer but continued to purr.

She leaned back against the wall and soon, with the warmth of the house coupled with petting the cat and feeling his vibration in her lap, Sloane closed her eyes and fell asleep.

29

Worries

THE NEXT MORNING SLOANE WAS FIRST AWARE OF THE MUFFLED chatter of her girls. Their voices sounded farther away than Sloane was comfortable with and then she heard the bing, dong, dinging sounds coming from what her consciousness told her was the piano in the far corner. *What harm could it do? Let the girls live a little,* her mind kept telling her. But in the end her practical side broke free from the side of her brain longing to fall into another sleep cycle. She lifted her hand to her eyes, rubbing them, then stretched.

Her knees ached from staying in the same crossed position all night and having slept in a sitting position, leaned against a brick wall, her muscles screamed at her for not finding a more comfortable position. Survival in middle age meant even more pain than normal.

The girls soon recognized their mom's yawns and they hurriedly paced back to her side.

"Good morning, Mom," Mae said, her voice husky and raw still.

She peeked at them kneeling in front of her. She smiled to see them somewhat happy, a clear difference from yesterday morning where they had to run for their lives at dawn. Sloane glanced at the fireplace and saw that someone had placed another log on the glowing embers.

"I put another log on," Wren said.

"Good," Sloane said and sat up, leaning forward away from the wall. She ached all over. Then she remembered the gray cat. Looking around the room, she asked, "Did you guys see the cat when you woke?"

They looked at each other. "No Mom," they said, shaking their heads. She was beginning to think they thought she was crazy.

"I swear that same gray cat came over and sat in my lap last night. He was purring and I fell asleep with him right here," she said pointing to her lap.

"No, we haven't seen a cat. Maybe he took off before we woke up?" Nicole offered.

"Yeah, maybe." She was starting to think the cat was a figment of her imagination. Perhaps she was *that* tired.

"What are we going to do today, Mom?" Wren asked.

"Well, I want you girls to remain inside while I check out the grounds and the other buildings," Sloane said.

"*Cough...cough.*" Nicole coughed.

"And *that's* why," Sloane said and ran her hand over Nicole's forehead to check for fever. Immediately she knew by the scorching touch of her skin that she did in fact have a fever running.

"Lie down, Nicole. Have you had water this morning?"

"Yes ma'am."

Then Sloane glanced at the other girls, knowing they too might be running temperatures. Wren looked fine but Mae's eyes were glossy and she knew right away that she too ran a temperature. *God, please help them,* she prayed to herself. Fevers were known to her now as the hallmarks of death after dealing with the pandemic, and it frightened her like nothing else.

After checking Wren as well, she was thankful she seemed to have escaped the grip of whatever it was the younger two were fighting. "You two need to relax and rest. Wren, let's see what we can find in the packs for breakfast and I'll start them on a fever reducer from our med kits. Thank God we still have that." She pulled the red med kit from her own pack while Wren riffled around in the girl's identical packs for another bottle of water and something suitable for breakfast.

"Mom, can we heat water over the fire to make the oatmeal packs?"

"Yes, let me see if I can find a kettle or something in the kitchen to heat the water in instead of using our little campfire pot."

She got up and stretched her legs, then reached for the ceiling and suddenly had the urge to go to the restroom. Then it dawned on her, "Did you guys go to the bathroom?"

Wren nodded and pursed her lips.

"Where?"

"In the bathroom," she pointed. "The way we did at home. I put a pot in there with a lid. I didn't think you'd want us going outside. How old is this place? The commode tank is near the ceiling."

"I'm sure it worked fine in its day. Then toilets were upgraded, kind of like your iPhone used to be."

She'd never considered using the indoor plumbing, assuming it was too old to work properly, and was glad Wren hadn't tried. Like an antique you only stare at and occasionally regard as a past symbol, you admire the beauty and ingenuity but you don't actually use it for its intended purpose.

Located in what she first thought was only a closet under the staircase was a tidy bathroom with a toilet and a pedestal sink. The angled room was so tiny she couldn't imagine having much else inside. She ducked her head as she entered and attempted to flip the old electric switch on the wall but of course nothing happened. It was a habit of times past; in dark rooms your hand automatically sought the switch on the inside wall. Instead, she left the door open a crack as she did her business and then opened it wider. She found it odd, looking at an antique bathroom and yet they were reduced to lesser means. Then she tried the water knob on the sink, doubting anything would happen, and a trickle of brackish water streamed out, staining the white porcelain an orangy rust color. Figuring her hands were cleaner than the water, she opted to use her sanitary wipes in her pack instead.

Her next mission was food. She passed by the room with the girls still hovering near the warmth from the fire. She could almost see her own breath this far into the house, where the heat had not yet penetrated. She checked outside and found that not only was it foggy but the grounds were a mess, strewn with wild branches scattered every where from the storm. The only way she could tell it was from a recent storm was from the gleaming emerald of the pine boughs that lay scattered in every conceivable direction atop the browner debris. She leaned over the kitchen sink to strain her vision through the outside window, hoping to at least come across Ace, even though she knew he was probably gone to them forever.

She backed away from the sink and looked around at the cupboards, wondering if they in fact contained anything at all. "Where would a kettle be?" she said to herself. Not wanting to disturb personal belongings, she thought perhaps the ones nearest the stove might be the first place to look and when she opened the old-time cupboard doors she found various cast iron pots and pans. Then she found a brass kettle perfect for their needs. "We're just borrowing this," she said to no one in particular. She took hold of the handle, and it was heavier than it looked.

She brought the kettle into the gray room and found the girls lying on their backs. Mae's hands were in the air while she formed different shapes with her fingers; she and Nicole were weaving stories together as children their age did. Sloane was thankful that even though their lives were in danger from the outside and from within they still found a glimpse of safe time to be children once again. It was a blessing to see and to hear their little chatter.

"Did you find something, Mom?" Wren asked, even though she saw her mother coming.

"Yes, I think this will work. The fire isn't really strong right now; we'll just scoot some of the embers over and fill it halfway with bottled water. We should have warm water in no time."

"Are there dishes and things in there? Does the stove work too?" Wren asked.

"I don't know. I'm sure the kitchen fireplace works well but there's no power. I mean, we could cook in there but I don't want to start more than one fire. This will work for now."

"We should put something over the hole in the door to keep the warm air inside," Wren reasoned.

"I don't think we can stay here long term, Wren," Sloane said, wanting to discourage her daughter from getting too settled.

"Why not? We have everything here. Shelter, and safety at least. They can't find us here," Wren reasoned.

"I'm not so sure. I hope that's true but we can't get too comfortable here. We need to have a plan if anyone comes around. We need a place to hide," she said as she used the fireplace poker to maneuver the fire around and added a level area to place the kettle on. She poured a whole bottle of water into the kettle, replaced the lid and sat it on the glowing embers, then pushed more of the red hot embers around the kettle and added another smaller log of wood.

"We'll need to find more water and dry wood. I'll check if there's any in the other buildings today."

"We could go outside and bring in some of the fallen branches in to dry and use," Nicole offered and then coughed.

Sloane smiled at her. "*You* are not going anywhere. You're sick," she said and felt her forehead that was even more feverish than it had been before. Both Mae and Nicole were beginning to show a fine mist of sweat over their faces.

Wren met her eyes and she had the same worried expression that she knew mirrored her own. They were stuck here for a while, at least until the girls were better. She only hoped they were safe for the time being.

"Let's remove some of these blankets for a bit," she said but Mae complained that she was cold and shivered when Sloane pulled them back. "I know, dove, but your fever is making you feel that way. We need to lower your temperature for a little bit and then I'll give them back to you, okay?"

She nodded her quivering chin and relinquished the covers, and Nicole did the same.

"How much bottled water do we have left?" Sloane asked Wren.

"We only have what's in our packs. We left most of it there," Wren said.

"Should we go back and try to get it?" Wren asked.

Sloane shook her head. "No way. I'll scout around after breakfast and see if there's a pump or something else we can use here."

"There's a tiny bit of water from the sink but it's orange and rusty," Nicole said through an increasingly scratchy voice.

"Yeah, maybe there's a well or a reservoir on the property. I don't know, I'll look around."

"We do have those water purifying tablets," Wren offered.

"We can also boil water," Sloane said and preferred that method over the awful taste the tablets left.

Soon, the kettle began to whistle, so Sloane used a t-shirt from her bag to wrap around the wooden handle and was careful since she injured the hand trying to punch the window pane open the day before. It still hurt but she didn't think anything was broken. It was the small miracles that helped her every day. She poured the contents of their oatmeal packets into four of the tin mugs from their packs and then poured inside a bit of the steaming water, just enough to reconstitute the oatmeal. Then she opted to use their plastic spoons and pulled out four of them. After a few minutes she stirred the goop that smelled a bit like brown sugar and maple syrup.

Handing one to each girl, Mae said, "Mmm…"

Even with their sore throats the oatmeal was a welcome treat. She hoped their stomachs could keep it down. So far it seemed to be just a throat ailment with a fever, probably brought on by the gas canisters the men used in their shelter. *What we've come to is this, the gassing of children to force them into a lie of compassion. There is no greater treachery than an entity marauding as saviors and perpetrators of anything but amnesty.*

After their meals were done, she cleaned up the dirty dishes by simply wiping them out with a damp towel.

Mae and Nicole's eyelids were dipping in a drowsy cadence. She hoped the meal and fever reducers would make them feel better but she needed to locate fresh water as soon as possible and for that she needed to explore the grounds.

"Are you okay to watch them, Wren, while I go look around?"

"Yes Mom, but please be careful. What would we do if you didn't come back?"

The question was an honest one; she needed to answer her. As she strapped on her weapon and zipped up her jacket she tried to formulate an answer. Though nothing came to her she decided to be as honest as possible. "Wren, if I knew the answer to that, we'd be doing it. So far, this is the safest place I can think of now. We're relatively hidden and the girls are sick; they can't run through the woods or make it long distances out in the elements." She shook her head. "No, we stay here for now unless something happens. Then we leave and look for another safe place to hide and bide our time. There is no scenario where I won't come back to you. Nothing will keep me away. Okay?" she said to her daughter, and it seemed good enough at least for now.

"Okay Mom."

Before she left, she let the girls have the thinest blanket to keep them covered. They were both fast asleep.

"I won't be gone long," she reassured her daughter, "and I'll look for something to cover the broken pane too." She took her backpack with all the empty bottles they had in hopes of finding a source of clean water. Wren locked the door behind her, though anyone could reach through and undo the lock.

"I'll be back to you soon," she said again and with her weapon drawn, Sloane stepped off the rickety wooden porch steps and down onto the soggy ground. She looked back at the door and Wren gave her a little farewell wave.

Sloane kept her index finger along the slide of her Glock, out and ready. She headed toward the largest of the outer buildings, what looked to her like an ancient barn built in the old way with the peaked roof, though even now, when most of these designs one saw far off in fields showed signs of sagging and dilapidation, from storms taking their toll, not so here. Somehow the building looked as if it could even be used today. Possibly built in the thirties or forties—she had no idea—surely there was a water source in a barn such as this? It must have at one time housed animals, she reasoned.

With each step her boots sank into the mud at least a quarter inch. The resent storms made the earth soggy and mucky. A few times she lifted her boot to squelching sounds and if she wasn't careful the wild grass would give way and she would slide a little. So while keeping a look out for any dangers she also had to leap at times from grass clump to grass clump in order to remain upright. The barn was situated on an incline and her thigh muscles ached a little by the time she reached the northwest corner.

The weathered barn's clapboard shingles looked as if they

needed a few new coats of stain, though the structure was as solid as any built today. She peeked around the building and then looked back to the house and saw no one, nothing around, so she walked toward the barn door entrance and attempted to pull the door back. It was locked. "Great," she said out loud.

Then she walked toward the east side and found that there was an addition she couldn't see before, built onto the side of the barn in the same style. There was a white front door and chimney and two windows on the front. "Does someone live here?" It certainly looked like living quarters, perhaps for the caretaker.

"Anyone here?" she called out low. There was no answer to her call. She walked up and opened the screened front door, knocked loudly and waited; no one came.

She let the screen door creak back into its latch and stepped off the stone step and looked at the ground. Her own footsteps were clear in the mud.

She continued to walk around, looking for a source of water and finding none. Then she heard, "MOM!" Wren was yelling out the back door and her heart lept in fear. She heeded no safety for herself but ran in the direction of Wren's scream. Something terrible was happening and as she descended the hill, she slid in the mud and landed on her rump but hastily made her self get up and run toward her children.

"What? What is it?" she asked, running up the steps.

"It's Nicole. I don't know...hurry!" Wren yelled in tears.

With her muddy boots on she ran through the kitchen and into the gray room to find Nicole shaking in convulsions. Mae sat by her side crying and holding Nicole's hand as she shook, unable to stop.

"It's okay, baby," Sloane said as she knelt by Nicole and pulled the girl to her side. She wiped her hair away from her face and felt how her fever raged.

"Oh God, please help her."

"What is it, Mom? What's making her do that?"

"She having convulsions, probably from the high fever. Quick, get some water and that t-shirt. Let's strip her clothes off and cool her down as quickly as we can."

Her skin was so warm. Sloane chastised herself for not thinking of how bad it was earlier. She shouldn't have left them.

"That's the last of our water mom," Wren said.

Sloane looked at the bottle and then disregarded her caution, using it all on Nicole. She soaked the t-shirt damp and then laid it across the child's bare chest, lifted it and laid it again on her lower extremities and continued the process over and over, then redampened the cloth and repeated the process. The convulsions stopped and with what little water remained in the water bottle. Sloane coaxed two more ibuprofen down her throat in hopes of lowering the temperature further. Once she was confident the fever was lessened she held up the empty bottle and then fear struck her as she looked across Nicole's body to Mae's glassy eyes staring back at her in fear.

She too was sick and most likely would have the same results as Nicole did. "Lie down, dear. No blankets for you either."

"What are we going to do, Mom?" Wren whispered.

"She's going to be fine, Wren. Her fever was just too high."

"I can go out and look for water," Wren offered.

"No! No," she nearly yelled at Wren. "We can use the liquid from some of the canned fruit we have for the next day or so. I'll try again later."

But later the wind picked up again and Sloane couldn't bear to leave the sick girls by themselves. Wren pulled all the fruit cans out of their packs and drained them of their liquid. She gave her sister another fever reducer and soon she too was off to a fevered sleep.

Sloane stared at the sticky amber liquid reserved in the containers. "Only two and half bottles. That might get us through until tomorrow."

"I don't need any, Mom," Wren said.

Sloane gave her a reassuring smile. Wren was known for being selfless. She patted her shoulder. "We'll find more tomorrow," she said.

"Please don't leave me with them, Mom. That was so scary. I didn't know what to do," Wren cried.

Sloane hugged her daughter, smelled her fear as she held her close. "Wren, you're a strong young woman. I know you are."

Wren shook her head against her mother's neck. "No, no, I'm not. I'm not strong like you, Mom. I'm so scared."

Sloane held her tighter. "Yes, you are, Wren. You're my daughter, I know you are. You've taken care of your little sister with no other adults around. You've done the right thing time and again. When I was lying in the road stabbed those months ago, you left shelter, against my instruction, because you knew it was the right thing to do. You've kept us safe. You can think on your own and that's what it takes. That's what bravery is, Wren. The ability to think in a time of crisis. You've proven that you're brave. I couldn't do any better than you, dear." She pulled her away a bit and looked into her swollen eyes, wiped the stray fringe from her forehead and smiled. "It's okay to be scared. I'm terrified most of the time. It's what you do when you're scared that counts."

Wren nodded and wiped her eyes. She looked to her sleeping sisters, for that was how she felt of Nicole also—a sister just like her own flesh and blood. "They're really sick, Mom. What are we going to do?"

Sloane took a deep breath. "Keep them hydrated and cool their bodies. Let them rest and keep what meds we have in them. Water is our first priority. If we'd only had time to grab that last bag...but we didn't and we can't dwell on it. There has to be potable water around here somewhere. This is a big farm; it must have its own well, cistern or water reservoir somewhere. If nothing else, I'll set some pans outside and if it starts to rain again, we can gather some fresh rain water."

"That's a good idea," Wren said with a spark in her eye. "I'll gather a few containers from the kitchen."

"I'll set them out. We can keep an eye on the girls for today and then I'll look around more tomorrow."

Wren rummaged around the old kitchen cabinets collecting containers suitable for collecting water while Sloane sat between the girls, watching them as they took each breath and cooled their extremities in intervals one after another until all the moisture in the rag had evaporated with their body heat.

"I'm ready, Mom," Wren said.

Sloane snapped herself out of her worried trance. She never thought she'd be in the position of needing water in all her days of growing up in the United States and now not only did she need it, her three children desperately needed clean water.

"I can do it, Mom. I can put the pans outside." Wren offered.

"No, no, I don't want you to go out there by yourself unarmed. There's another little house built onto the barn. I didn't get a chance to check it out but we may not be the only people here. Let's be very careful when we're outside. You can stand at the door and hand them to me. I need to place them where there's no tree cover for the cleanest water catch."

"Okay," Wren replied.

Sloane put her coat back on and reluctantly left the girls' side. By this time, night descended rapidly and cloaked all in darkness, coming more as a comfort than a threat. She stacked several tin pots and pans together and crept out in the dark, holding them in one bear hug and her weapon in the other; vigilance was an old friend by now.

As her boots squelched in the mud again, she watched her footing and carefully laid down the pots in hopes for rain to arrive once again. It never seemed far off this time of year.

Then she backed her steps again the way she came and retrieved a second armload from Wren, waiting by the door.

"Okay, that should be enough," Sloane said.

And when she'd placed those containers down as well, she stood for moment in the dark, watching the night for any movement or any light. Other than a cold breeze nothing was apparent, but she felt someone there watching them. A notion passed that perhaps it was the cat, eyeing her from inside one of the outbuildings.

"Mom," Wren said from the doorway.

She turned to her daughter.

"Nicole's awake."

Sloane left the watchful stare while she returned to their haven to check on the child that was now hers out of circumstance but loved all the same.

If something were to happen to any of them, she couldn't imagine moving forward from the pain. It couldn't happen, not this time. She would never let it happen.

Once inside the doorway, she removed her boots and locked the door, not that it mattered with the window broken.

It was freezing outside and barely tolerable inside. She opted to keep the fire down for the girls to lower their temperatures.

She went to Nicole's side. "Hi darling." Her eyes were glassy and barely open. "How are you feeling?"

"Throat...hurts," was all the child could make audible.

"I wonder if it's something like strep throat?" Wren asked, looking pained.

Sloane felt Nicole's forehead again and though it was hot it wasn't as warm as before. "Do you think you can sip a little juice?"

Nicole nodded, opting out of saying anything because of the pain.

Sloane lifted her head up from the pillow and held a little glass of canned juice to her chapped lips. Nicole sipped it down a little at a time. Then Sloane held out a capsule out for her to take. "You need to swallow this with the next sip,"

Nicole shook her head. "Huurts," she croaked out.

"I know, dove, but you must. There's no choice. Can you do this for me?"

Nicole looked as if she could cry but nodded.

"Good girl. It won't be easy but it will help you. You trust me, right?"

Nicole nodded again.

"Okay, here you go." She placed it between her lips and then held out the amber liquid for her again to take a big sip. Nicole swallowed and then nodded again to Sloane that it went down.

"Okay, good girl." She laid her down on her side. "Try to sleep more. That's the best thing for you both."

Nicole smiled at her and closed her eyes again. Sloane hoped she didn't remember the convulsions from earlier. What a terror to remember such a thing.

Sloane's eyes met Wren's and she could see how worried her daughter was; no doubt she thought the same things.

"Why don't you go into the next room and gather the firewood by the fireplace. We'll need it for tonight. There is some in the kitchen as well."

"Okay."

Sloane thought it would do her daughter some good to take a short walk away from her sick siblings in order to breathe a little and worry a little less. Doing something constructive might help her too. And besides that, every room in the house was an adventure of its own. Wren grabbed her flashlight and had her weapon on her side just like her mom. Soon she came back with wide eyes, bearing an armful of firewood. "This place is huge," she whispered.

"It is. I haven't even checked it all out yet."

"Did you see all the paintings? How old is this place?"

"I have no idea," Sloane said as she stacked the firewood.

As soon as she was freed from the first load, Wren scurried off to gather the next load. When she returned so did the astonishment in her eyes. Sloane had lost that look as soon as she discovered the girls were really sick and in the course of her worry over their need for water.

They went through the same process twice more and Sloane concluded they probably had enough for the next few days.

Then she and Wren had a small meal of peanut butter crackers from their packs and Sloane let Wren take the first watch so that she could sleep a few hours.

When she woke, Wren went to sleep, and then she took a walk to the kitchen with the knit shirt she used earlier to check and see if there was any way to soak the rag again so that she could wipe the fevered girls down to cool their skin.

Peeking out the window, she saw there was at least some snow that had fallen, so she went out and picked up one of the tin vessels and scooped up more of the snow to bring inside. As it melted by the fire, she soaked the cloth and again blotted the girls' skin in intervals to help lower their temps. Mae, at least, had not gone into convulsions but she was still just as hot as before. At one point, Sloane was able to melt more snow and woke the child to give her more medication and helped her swallow some of the liquid.

Then they were all asleep again and Sloane was left with her thoughts, her worries and what they might do to help their predicament. And in the dark, she spotted a pair of green eyes staring back out at her. Nearly startled into screaming, she caught herself. "Hello kitty. Where have you been all day? You know, they think I'm crazy and just imagining you," she said to the cat as he curled up into her lap. She ran her hand down his back and then noticed something new. Where there had been no collar before, there was a worn brown leather one now and it held a rolled-up piece of paper, tied on one end. "What's this?"

She slid it out and uncurled a ripped piece of paper. On the note was written, "There is clean water at the pump, behind the barn." It was signed, "A friend."

She was suddenly struck with terror. There *was* someone here after all, and they knew of her presence here on the farm. Sloane's heart beat out of her chest; even though it was signed 'a friend' it made her no less frightened.

Looking at her girls as they slept, she felt helpless to save them. At dawn's light she would have to wake them and make them run again. That's what they needed to do but how could she move the sick girls? It was an impossible situation and one she had no answers for. If only her Finn where here, she thought for the millionth time. *He would know what to do. He would know how to keep us safe. God, I miss him more than ever.*

Soon she drifted off to sleep and the cat stepped out of her lap at the first rise of dawn, padded lightly over the sick children, sniffing here and there, and then disappeared back the way he came.

30

Encounters

EARLY THE NEXT MORNING, BEFORE THE GIRLS EVEN STIRRED, Sloane snuck out of the house through the back kitchen door to see that the pots were generally empty; only little rivers of water leaned in the curvature of their lowest depths. Most of the meager snowfall had long melted into the mud.

The girls were fevered and they needed more than the mouthful she could accumulate had she decided to pour each container's worth into one glass. Determined, she gathered up all of their empty water bottles inside her backpack and grabbed one of the larger containers from the ground where it sat. With her Glock in hand, she would make this a quick and successful trip to the pump the stranger said was on the other side of the barn. Of course, she knew whomever it was would watch her every move and perhaps it was a trap, but it was a chance she had to take. The girls were sick and she had to take the chance.

She found herself running quickly and in near-panic across the hill toward the far end of the barn. She glanced back once at the house before it was out of sight. Now she was having second thoughts about having not awakened Wren before she left but it was too late for that now; there was no turning back.

When she reached the side of the enormous old barn, her chest heaved with the cold air stinging her throat. She laid herself flat against its surface and looked around, weapon raised. She peeked around the back corner ever so carefully. And there it was, a purple bucket against an old-timey pump.

She looked to the woods and thought that if there was someone there, she'd never see them. Then, terrified that it might be a trap set by the soldiers, her legs shook with fear while in her mind, she tried to calm herself, logically reasoning that it was just someone else trying to hide from them too. Her muddy boot inched forward. She made herself move slowly in case of any movement, watching as though this were her last stand, and any minute measured shift would send her into a fight to the death. Then she took cautious steps out in the early morning dawn. Footfall after footfall, her boots crunched the frozen grass beneath her. Only twenty feet away she continued to scan every possible angle until she stood on the broken concrete of the pump platform.

A large purple bucket at her feet was already half full with glorious water. Only a small circle of ice floated like a crystal island within the tiny ocean. Such a precious life source so abundant, yet so far away when desperate for a wet drop. Immediately she knelt and began to submerge the empty water bottles in her backpack while continuing to search her surroundings for any sign of an attacker.

When she was done with that task, having filled ten bottles, she pushed the bucket out of the way and then stood and lifted the lever for the pump and began wrenching the handle down once, twice and a third time then cold water gushed from the spigot into her container. Some of it splashed outside and she thought herself wasteful. Finally, it was almost too full to carry and she wondered how she would be able to hold her gun and carry the pot at the same time. There was no way to do it well; she'd have to make a decision—holster the weapon and carry the pot with two hands with the backpack on her shoulders.

She took another hard look all around her and decided to take the chance and reluctantly holstered her weapon. Then she donned the loaded backpack and knelt down to lift the full container of water. She didn't want to have to come back for more later, so she reasoned that she only wanted to do this once today. She started hurrying down the crusty grass when she heard a male voice call out to her, "Hello!"

Startled and terrified, she slipped on the frozen grassy hill. The pot of water turned toward her in that moment as she reached to brace her fall, and two gallons of water landed on her chest as she lay on her back on the frozen ground, drenching her chest entirely.

She twisted to her side as a dark shape began to approach her and wrenched her Glock from her holster. Her damp and dripping hair covered her face so that her vision was obscured.

"I'm sor..." the voice began.

"Don't come closer!"

"I won't, I won't."

When her vision cleared, a man stood only ten feet from her with his hands in the air.

"I swear to God, I'm not here to hurt you."

"I don't care who you swear to. If you take one step toward me, I'll kill you."

"Look, I'll even back up three paces. I just see that you got my note. I thought I'd introduce myself."

"I don't care who you are. I have sick children or we would have left already. I need to get them well and then we'll leave, I promise. Just please give me a few more days."

"I'm not trying to kick you out. I saw you ladies come in

during the storm. You're welcome to stay here. It's pretty safe. No one has come around here yet."

"Are you the caretaker?"

"Well, sort of. I'm the second cousin of the guy that haunts that house." He pointed toward the house with a raised finger. He was trying to be funny and she sort of believed him.

"It's not haunted."

"Whatever you say. It's creepy enough. Look, I'm a doctor. I came out here to check on my mom's place on my way to Portland and just happened to be here when the wave hit. I can take a look at your girls. I'm an internal medicine doctor."

She moved the damp hair away from her face and studied him for a moment. He was tall man with light brown hair and even in these times he wore what you'd expect to see a doctor wearing, a mildly plaid button-up shirt and through the v of his neck she could see a crisp white undershirt. His jacket wasn't one for the rugged outdoors but one a doctor would wear over his shirt in cold weather. He was clean-shaven even still, with only a hint of a shadow on his face. He wore dark wash jeans and had on expensive leather hiking boots. She knew the type, career driven. He was handsome and said all the right things so far, but she could never trust him. She glanced at the pot on the ground but still held him at gunpoint. "No, that's okay." She began to move away from him and farther down the hill toward the house and her children.

"I swear to you, I'm a friend. It's only me here. I haven't even talked with anyone since this began."

"Look, I don't need your help. I just need a few more days here to get my girls well and then we'll leave." She continued a few more steps away.

He nodded. "Okay, stay as long as you need to. Seriously, it's just me and I would never hurt you. If you need me to look at your daughters, I'm right here. Just knock on the door."

She glanced at him like he was crazy.

"You sure you don't want to refill the water?" he asked, pointing at the empty pot.

Now she was annoyed and drenched. "I have enough for now," she said and pointed toward her backpack.

"Okay," he said, getting the hint, and backed away with a charming smile on his face.

She lowered her gun and stalked back to the house, knowing he watched her every more.

31

Chances

"Did you feed Sally?" Mae said in what Sloane feared was delirium. She was thrashing with her fever and making statements that had no bearing on their current situation. It worried her even more. She'd already used half the water she brought with her and had given each of the girls medication to lower their fever but nothing helped.

"Mom, we have to do something more. This isn't working," Wren cried while rocking back and forth on her knees beside her sister.

Sloane hovered over both girls. Nicole had already gone through another convulsive event and barely became conscious enough to swallow water and the medication that Sloane coaxed down her throat.

"What else can we do?" Wren implored.

Sloane rubbed a hand through her hair in frustration. She held her palm over her mouth considering her only alternative. It was a risk and she hated to take it but like Wren said, they were running out of options.

"Wren, I'm going to go and get the doctor I told you about earlier."

"The stranger? Mom, no!"

"I don't know what else to do. They're getting worse, not better. We have to take a chance on him."

"Okay, okay. Please hurry back. I'm afraid what will happen when you're gone."

Sloane put on her coat and kissed the top of Wren's head. "I'll be right back, okay?"

"Okay, Mom. Hurry."

Then Sloane didn't dare look back. The darkness had descended hours ago and she held her weapon tight as she ran again from the back door to the living quarters on the side of the barn.

She barely knocked when he opened the door. He held a paperback book in one hand and the ambient light of the fireplace glowed around him. "Is there something wrong?" he asked with concern etched on his face.

"I wouldn't be here otherwise. Please, can you come and look at my girls? Their fever…I can't get it down." And in shame Sloane was horrified that tears were springing from her eyes and streaming down her cheeks. She wiped them away as quickly as she could. She couldn't help their persistent descent.

"I'll grab my bag," he said and left the door ajar while he disappeared inside for a moment, trusting her when she would never trust him. He showed back up momentarily with one arm inside a jacket. In his hand he held a canvas bag.

He ushered her off the porch and they walked quickly back to the main house. "How long have they been running a temp?"

All the days seemed to scramble together. "A few days now?"

"Did they have a cold or a virus before you left?"

"They…were inside a hideout when soldiers threw in these

smoke bombs. It killed our dogs but I got to the girls in time to pull them out. I think it's related to that somehow."

"Okay, and that was two to three days ago?"

"Yes." He was clearly in doctor mode now. She hated it how doctors demanded to know down to the day you started your period or the first day of a virus event, etc.... "It started off with a sore throat and then a fever." They reached the back door and as they entered Wren stared back at the tall stranger in their midst. "This is my daughter Wren. She was also in the bunker when the gas struck but it didn't affect her as badly."

"Hi Wren. I'm Dr. Kent. You don't need to be scared. I won't harm you or your sisters."

Wren just stared and nodded at him but she was clearly still very protective of her sisters.

Dr. Kent came forward with his sight locked on the jumble of blankets in the gray room, intermixed with two feverish girls.

"Mom," Nicole said.

Wren looked to Sloane and said, "She keeps calling to her mom."

Sloane held her palm over her mouth again. She had to get hold of herself. Getting emotional right now was the last thing that would help their circumstances.

In a very calming tone, Dr. Kent explained, "Sometimes when our fevers are so high we tend to hallucinate and dream. It's the brain coping with the high fever."

Wren nodded as if understanding why they were talking about deceased loved ones helped her cope with the worry of possibly losing her sisters to death's grip.

He opened his bag and took out a thermometer. He held it up to the light and shook the mercury down. "Back to the basics. My electronic one broke," he said with a smile. "Wren, could you remove their blankets?" Sloane assumed he was trying to give Wren something to do in order to help *her* cope with the situation.

Sloane continued to stand behind the man, watching him closely. She wanted to trust him but was no longer capable of believing the best of any man. Nothing was left to chance when it came to her daughters. She stood even as the man worked with her hand over her Glock, though it appeared to her that the doctor before her wasn't even armed, as far as she knew.

"Well, I'm not sure what caused it but it certainly sounds like pneumonia," he said after he removed his stethoscope from Nicole's chest. "Both of them." His look was grim and pensive. "I'm afraid they need round-the-clock care. You shouldn't take them anywhere. I've seen cases like this and it takes weeks to recover." He held his hands up. "I swear I'm not giving you a line. I've got antibiotics to give them but even with those, this will take time to recover from. You can't take them anywhere for a while, I hope you understand that. Neither of them will be able to stand for long periods of time, let alone walk for days, even if they start to recover from this tonight. The first thing we need to do is lower their temperature. Do you trust me enough to let me help them?"

Not feeling as if she had much choice in the matter she said, "Can you?" But he was suddenly distracted from answering when Nicole again went into convulsions. Her young body was so wracked by fever her brain went into shock trying to relieve itself. He gently slipped his hand behind her sweat-covered head and then tilted her onto her side. Then he looked to Wren's startled face and said gently, "It started to snow earlier and I saw the pots outside. Could you please gather one of them, or perhaps two if you can manage it?"

Wren scurried away and he turned his attention to Sloane while he held Nicole as she went through the seizing. "I didn't want to say this in front of your older daughter but...they could die. This is serious. I can't promise you that I can see them through this but I'll try."

Sloane had not removed her eyes from Nicole in what looked like the throes of death. "Please, please help them."

Wren returned with the pails of snow and he acted quickly. Taking off their clothes and packing the snow around them, he let it melt and soak into their blankets underneath them. He emptied the first pail and then handed it to Sloane. "Keep them coming. We have to cool them down quickly."

She ran to the back door, soon followed by Wren doing the same task.

A short time later, both girls looked as if they were making snow angels in the gray room with the white snow packed between their extremities and full buckets to replace what snow melted from their body heat.

He took their temperatures again and both girls showed improvement. "It's not enough. We need to keep it up until it's at least lower than 103 degrees. Let's get more water into them and I'll slip in the antibiotic."

"We need more water," Wren said.

He looked to Sloane, imploring her to trust him alone with the girls. "It's okay, I'll go get more. Just keep an eye on them."

"No, it's okay. I'll go." She looked to Wren. "You can come with me so you know where it is."

"It's safe. I promise. I haven't had any problems here," Dr. Kent said.

Sloane nodded. She couldn't help herself looking back at him once more as she left him alone with her daughters. She was taking a chance and it scared her more than anything. She couldn't help but run again up the slope to the barn. Wren picked up on her sense of urgency and hurried as well.

"I think he's okay, Mom," Wren said.

A thousand responses flew through her brain but none of them would work well. "Just hurry," she said as she ran out of options.

What's he going to do? She reasoned. *Take off with two sick girls while I run out to get them water from the well? It's fine, it's fine, it's fine...* she told herself over and over as she flew through filling the bottles with water that mostly flowed over the spout. When they finished filling the ten bottles, Sloane remembered falling down the frozen grass earlier and warned her daughter, "Don't run here. You might fall."

They slid down the hill and continued running, holding five bottles each. Once back at the house, Sloane couldn't help herself. She bolted inside and found him sitting in the exact same position beside Mae's side, checking her pulse with his finger to her neck.

"She's fine, that is, they're doing slightly better. Temperatures are dropping, so that's good. Do you have dry blankets for them once we get their temps down?"

She shook her head as she handed him the first cool water bottle. "No, that's all we had. We had to leave almost everything. I found these upstairs but that's all I could find."

"It's okay, I've got extra blankets in the cabin. I'll go back and get them soon. Or you can. They're in a chest at the end of the bed," he offered.

"Actually, I think there are more upstairs in the bedrooms. Wren, can you take the flashlight and go see what you can find?"

"Sure," she said as Sloane handed her the flashlight.

When she was out of earshot, Dr. Kent cautioned. "You sure you want her to wander around this house? I swear it *is* haunted."

She stared into his hazel eyes and she thought perhaps he was serious. Perhaps he was trying to make their situation lighter with humor. She appreciated the effort but still, she hoped it was only his wit showing. "This house isn't haunted, it's perfect—a little dusty but perfect."

"Sure, have it your way," he said. "I'm telling you, my mom always warned me that her cousin still roams these halls looking for his wife."

She scoffed. How in the world could he make her feel less

tense at a time like this? Soon, the sound of someone running down the steps caught her attention.

"See, here he comes."

She shook her head at him as Wren hurried into the room, sheet-white but holding a stack of blankets in her arms.

"Are you okay?" she asked, taking the dry blankets from her daughter's arms.

"Yeah," she huffed, out of breath. "It's scary up there. Everything's so old but in perfect condition and it's dark, creepy," she shuddered.

"See, I told you," Dr. Kent said to Sloane.

"That doesn't mean the house is haunted," Sloane said.

"Mm-hmm," he said as he packed more snow around the girls.

A short time later, he checked the girls' vitals again and looked to Sloane. "They're doing better but I think I should keep an eye on them tonight, here. Is that okay with you?"

"Yes, please."

"Look, I slept well last night but you look as if you're going to fall over any minute." Before she could protest he held up a hand to stall her. "I know you don't trust me but you need to sleep. You're no good to them exhausted. I swear to God, I won't go anywhere. I need to monitor their vitals every hour and push fluids whenever I get a chance. You two can make a pallet closer to the fireplace to stay warm."

Wren already yawned at the prospect of sleeping, causing Sloane to automatically repeat the gesture. *Darn it!* She was just going to deny her sleepiness when the yawn irresistibly overcame her.

"See? Look, I'm not armed. I mean you no harm. I'm only here to help you. You can open your eyes and you'll see me right here. There's nothing to worry about, I promise you. I won't let anything happen to you here."

There was no way she was going to trust those words but she needed to sleep and he had given her no reason to distrust him so far. He was right in one regard: if she didn't sleep soon, she was going to fall over. She'd only slept a few hours in the whole time they'd been there.

"Okay, but only for a little while. I'll wake up in a few hours and then you can get some sleep too."

He laughed a little in a way that made her comfortable. "That would be nice. Hey, I know your name is Wren," he pointed at the teen. "What's your name?" he asked Sloane.

"It's Sloane. Sloane McKenna."

Then Wren asked him, "We know your name is Dr. Kent but what's your first name?"

"Phineas. You can call me Finn," he said and then wondered why her face suddenly went blank.

"That...that was my Dad's name," Wren said.

"I'm...so sorry. Did he pass recently?"

Sloane listened to the conversation intently though she hadn't responded as she set up a pallet for both her and her daughter. Her stomach clenched at the mention of her dear deceased husband's name. She looked at him, startled.

Wren replied in a quiet voice after glancing at her mother, "No, he died during the pandemic. He was a science teacher. I miss him very much." She looked sad but a little smile at his remembrance too.

It comforted Sloane to know her daughter was healing over her father's death. The event was such a horrible heartache for them all, and what took place after his death—she'd never forgive herself for putting her girls through it all.

"Well, I'm very sorry to hear that Wren. I can tell he was a great man because I can see that in you. I'm sure he was very proud of you."

Wren's smile deepened. The conversation warmed Sloane's heart, and why? She wasn't sure. Just that those words were something her daughter needed to hear from someone other than herself.

"You can call me Kent if you'd like. If...it would be easier, that is," he offered.

"That's okay," Wren said as she made herself comfortable under the covers. "You remind me of him anyway. I always just called him Dad, so it's no problem. Goodnight."

Sloane couldn't believe her ears. Her daughter hardly strung five words together and never spoke to strangers even when the world was sort of normal, and here she was carrying on what would be considered an extended conversation with this handsome stranger. Sloane looked up at the man. He was staring right at her, more like through her. She didn't know what to think. Dr. Kent's face bore a caring and sympathetic expression; he probably felt sorry for their situation. She didn't want his sympathy. She wanted her girls better and safe. If she could believe this man that carried her dead husband's name, they were safe here. But she wasn't going to trust him, not yet anyway; that would take a long, long, time.

Before she gave into the gravity pulling her eyelids down, she laid her head on her makeshift pillow and rolled onto her side, staring at him. "Do you mind if *I* call you Kent? I just couldn't bear to use Finn's name."

"*You* can call me whatever you want," he said and when he smiled a dimple appeared on the side of his handsome face.

She rolled her eyes and slept.

32

Ghosts

THE NEXT MORNING, SHE WOKE TO CHATTERING. SUN RAYS beamed across her eyelids through the curtains. Before she even opened her eyes, she could tell it was a freezing cold but bright and sunny day.

Then she realized the chattering voice was Nicole's, though still hoarse. She sat up quickly and four sets of eyes landed on her. "Nicole, Mae?"

Both girls smiled at her.

"They're fine, Mom," Wren said.

"Well, they're better but not out of the woods," Kent said.

She couldn't help herself; she cried. "Why didn't you wake me?" she asked as she scrambled over to them. Kent had them sitting side by side against the couch, bundled in dry blankets and sipping water while nibbling on soda crackers.

Wren looked to Kent and smiled. "Mom, no one could wake

you up." She laughed, and Sloane hadn't seen her daughter this relaxed in a very long time.

"You're a hard sleeper. We've been sitting here for hours getting to know one another."

"He puts people to sleep for a living," Mae said. "Isn't that weird?" She giggled.

He'd charmed them, Sloane thought. He healed them but he charmed them too. She wasn't sure she liked that.

He looked at her silently and seriously for a time. Then he said, "I think you guys are good for a few hours. Why don't I go back to my place and take a nap, get cleaned up and I'll come back and check on you? Does that sound okay?"

Her first thought was that he was probably running from them. He'd probably disappear. It didn't bother her. She and the girls were a lot of responsibility in a time like this and she didn't want him around anyway; she didn't need him. She smiled and agreed, "Sure, thank you Kent. I don't know what I would have done without you."

He stood and she shook his outstretched hand. It looked like goodbye to her. He had no responsibility to her and the girls; she couldn't blame him for running away. They were too much of a responsibility for anyone to take on.

"They'll need more ibuprofen in another hour but the fever is staying relatively low now. Keep drinking water and take little bites," he said to them without really meeting Sloane's eyes again.

"No running up and down the stairs," he said to them, "and mind the ghost." The girls giggled again.

"I'm not kidding." He acted incredulous. "No one believes me."

She watched him put on his jacket and tie his boots, and then he left. She was sure that was goodbye and they'd never see his handsome and charming face again but it didn't matter; he'd helped them when they truly needed someone the most and she'd be forever grateful.

She smiled at the girls laughing around her. She thanked God for him, bringing her this peace when she needed help the most.

33

Trust

AFTER THE GIRLS WOKE FROM THEIR SECOND NAP OF THE DAY, Sloane gave them more of the medication that Kent had left for them. They were feeling so much better and even managed to eat an MRE apiece from their packs. She'd cleaned up the wet clothing and sopped up all the melted snow while the girls napped. She had the fire going nicely when Wren asked, "Where's Finn? Is he coming back?"

Sloane felt sorry to break her daughter's heart. It would be one of many lessons to learn with men in her young life. "I don't think we'll see Dr. Kent again, dove. But it was so nice of him to help us out when he did. He didn't have to."

Her daughter was silent for a time, thinking no less, that what Sloane foretold was coming true. He was gone and though they felt a little more secure with him there, it was a feeling they could not get used to. They could never trust anyone; recent events had taught them that and the sooner the girls learned this lesson the better off they would be.

If they were the lenders of hearts, they would soon learn to fall, and that was a lesson she couldn't help them learn; only strangers would teach them that and Kent had done her a favor in not only helping the girls get better but also learning this little lesson.

A few hours later, the girls were asleep. With her eyes transfixed on the fire flames, she was a little startled when there was a knock on the back door.

She cautiously approached with her Glock out. She looked out the window and immediately flung open the door. "Ace!" she yelled and the black dog jumped into her lap, licking her and jumping all over.

"Does this guy belong to you guys?" Kent asked. "He would not go away."

"Yes!" she said, loving her furry friend.

"I found him sniffing around the water pump and watched him run back and forth like he was looking for a familiar scent. Sorry I slept so long. I was more tired than I realized," he said, rubbing his hand through his crazy hair.

Her eyes met his.

He smiled.

She thought, *Please prove me wrong...*

AFTERWORD

To be among the first to learn about new releases, announcements, and special projects, please go to AuthorARShaw.com to join my newsletter.

OTHER WAYS TO KEEP UP TO DATE:

Follow me on Amazon

Follow me on BookBub

Please write a review Dawn of Deception on Amazon.com; even a quick word about your experience can be helpful to prospective readers. The author welcomes any comments, feedback, or questions at Annette@AuthorARShaw.com.

ACKNOWLEDGMENTS

No work of fiction comes to fruition without the helpful hands of others.

For this novel, I'd like to thank Dr. Vonda for her clear and concise editing. Cheryl Nelson Deariso for her keen eye in proofreading. Hristo Argirov Kovatliev for his mad skills in cover art. And never last, and certainly not least, my faithful BETA readers with whom my polished novels are never without.

Personally, I'd like to thank my Dad for his constant support, my son for sticking by me in the worst of times, and Henry my cat, (we rescued each other).

ABOUT THE AUTHOR

What the world dreads most has happened...is the tagline A. R. Shaw writes under and that statement gives you an idea of where her stories often lead...into the abyss of destruction and mayhem with humanity thrown in as a complication. She writes realistic scenarios which are often the worries we think of in the dark of night.

So far she's sold over 51 thousand books and only just begun. A. R. Shaw resides somewhere in the Pacific Northwest.

ALSO BY A. R. SHAW

The Graham's Resolution series

The China Pandemic
The Cascade Preppers
The Last Infidels
The Malefic Nation
The Bitter Earth

※

Surrender the Sun

Bishop's Honor
Sanctuary
Point of No Return

※

The French Wardrobe

Made in the USA
Coppell, TX
25 June 2021